The Staked Plains

When buffalo-hide hunter, Quentin McLeod, rescues Carlotta Mainord from Comanche raiders, their struggle is still far from over. They must face further hostility from the Indians, flash floods and white brigands, only to find themselves in even greater danger when they arrive in the apparent safety of New Mexico.

Carlotta Mainord is attacked and left helpless in a coma and McLeod is blamed and accused of being a Comanchero. Can he convince the hanging jury of his innocence and will he escape the lynch mob in time?

The Staked Plains

BILLY MOORE

A Black Horse Western

ROBERT HALE · LONDON

ISBN 978-0-7090-8813-4

Robert Hale Limited
Clerkenwell House
Clerkenwell Green
London EC1R 0HT

www.halebooks.com

Typeset by
Derek Doyle & Associates, Shaw Heath
Printed in Great Britain by
the MPG Books Group, Bodmin and King's Lynn

ONE

It was the wind shift that made Quentin McLeod take action. The wind shifted to his back and blew as hard as it usually did on the High Plains. The Comanches' horses couldn't fail to smell him and his horse. Without consciously thinking about what to do, he fished a match out of his pocket and scratched it across his tightly stretched woolen pants.

He took a moment to light a small, dark cigar and admire the pink morning sky beyond the mouth of the canyon. Quail chattered nervously to each other, disturbed that all these humans were interrupting their morning watering. An eagle soared high over the mouth of the canyon.

McLeod took a deep drag and savored the strong Mexican tobacco, then touched the match to a twist of dry grama grass and inhaled appreciatively again while the grama grass blazed up. The big hide-hunter liked the mixed smells of the two smokes. When he touched the torch to the dead cedars behind which he had been hiding, the dry needles exploded like gunpowder. The wind gusting from directly behind him drove the flames toward the Comanches. Quickly he shook burning blades of grass into tinder-dry cedar boughs across a wider front.

Fire raged like stampeding buffalo toward the Comanches. The warriors and Comanchero abandoned everything and scrambled desperately up the nearest rocks to escape the sudden death racing down upon them.

McLeod grabbed a handful of mane and swung on to his big buckskin. He took a moment to wrap an old shirt as a blinder around the horse's eyes then dug his spurs into his horse's side. The big buckskin barreled down the narrow pathway by which McLeod had entered this concealed pocket the night before.

McLeod watched the woman stare death calmly in the eye as the fire approached. He removed the blindfold from the buckskin, used his spurs again and raced toward her. The woman moved as close to his path as her bonds permitted and stood with her bound hands extended.

The big buckskin's eyes rolled in panic. McLeod controlled the terrified animal with one hand and, with the other, whipped out a razor-sharp skinning knife to slash the rawhide thongs that bound the captive's hands.

The tall woman wasted no time. As McLeod reached out his arm, she caught his hand and vaulted agilely up behind him. She hung on to McLeod and the back of the panic-stricken horse as it bolted wildly toward the opening of the canyon; this woman could *ride*, McLeod realized. Both smelled rather than felt their own hair singeing; cedar boughs exploded wildly into flame. Neither had time to fret about smoke burning their lungs.

McLeod felt the woman rip his pistol from its holster. Before he could react, fire and smoke erupted beside him. A Comanche he hadn't seen tumbled down from a ledge along the side of the Cap Rock. The woman, Quentin McLeod realized, was either an excellent shot or lucky.

Either trait would be appreciated.

Ahead, just outside the mouth of the canyon, McLeod saw the long-legged bay that the Comanchero had ridden, the two pack mules' lead ropes still tied to the back of the horse's saddle. He veered toward the horse and the woman swung easily from the rump of McLeod's horse on to the bay's saddle before the buckskin ever came to a full stop.

McLeod slashed the mules' lead lines but noticed that they broke into a trot following the bay. He hesitated. Their chances of eluding the Comanches for several hundred miles back to the Texas settlements were slim. The Comanches would quickly recover and catch the scattered horses. By switching to fresh horses regularly, they would eventually overcome even the two superb animals on which McLeod and the woman were mounted. He made his decision and turned south.

The two rode hard without talking for the next five miles, neither missing the opportunity to appraise the other surreptitiously. McLeod's initial impression that the woman was beautiful proved true. She was taller than most women, standing, McLeod guessed, only a couple of inches less than his six feet. Her most striking feature was the deep blue color of her eyes, as deeply blue as the wild indigo with which her now tattered dress had probably been dyed. The blue eyes were especially striking because they were so unexpected in one with a deep olive complexion and raven-black hair. He quickly came to look forward to her habit of throwing her long and unruly curls back out of her eyes with an impudent toss of her head.

At a small trickle of reddish water, McLeod halted his horse and dismounted while Buck drank. The woman stayed on the bay but let it drink alongside Buck. McLeod checked the bay's hoofs and grunted his satisfaction to see fresh shoes. It seemed he could feel the woman cringe as he stood close to her legs, but perhaps it was his imagination.

He tried to think of things to say to her but found himself tongue-tied as he often was around women. 'What's your name?' he finally managed and winced inwardly at the unintendedly harsh tone of his voice.

'Carlotta,' she answered. Her eyes drifted to the old US Cavalry uniform pants he was wearing, and turned sharply away.

He stumbled for words. 'I'm McLeod,' he finally grunted in a hard voice.

The woman, Carlotta was the name he reminded himself, didn't look back into his eyes. At last he swung back into his saddle and turned away without speaking another word.

This man was considerably thicker in the chest than her late husband, Grady Mainord, who had been reckoned a big man even in Texas, Carlotta noticed as she rode out of the fire on the back of his big buckskin. Little else about his appearance made much of an impression on her, except that he wore an old pair of the blue-and-yellow-legged uniform pants of the US Cavalry, still hated in Texas two years after the war had ended. Like most men away from town, his face was covered with a tangle of whiskers, light-brown flecked with highlights of red and blond.

His once brown, flat-crowned Stetson was now faded to the color of the red dust of the High Plains; sweat stained it above its snake-hide band. Any girl from the Texas ranch country would notice that his bull-hide boots were so scuffed and run-over at the heels that most twenty-dollar-a-month cowhands would have given up on them before now. His leather jacket had turned dark from wear, smoke, grease and weather.

Her arms had almost rebelled at pulling herself close to the scroungy garment when she had ridden behind him. But her face flushed hot when she remembered how tightly she had hugged against him, liking the smooth yet powerful rippling and flowing of his muscles in the desperate exertion of the moment. She had delayed longer than necessary before pulling away.

The sun was now well into the sky. To the east, grassy plains rolled as far as the eye could see. To the west, a continuous clay wall that must be a thousand feet high marked what Carlotta knew must be the edge of the Staked Plains. Prickles ran up and down her back as she thought of stories of these Staked Plains as the stronghold of the Comanche and Kiowa. Being so close to it affected her like discovering a coiled rattlesnake near her feet.

Carlotta thought back to the man in black who had arrived at the camp by the water hole, obviously a Comanchero. Never had she felt so strongly that she was in the presence of evil – his pallid skin, the strange-looking hands, but mostly those eyes. Her skin crawled as she remembered the brush of his cold, hard fingers against her face. And what had he called her? *Juliette.* He had muttered the name Juliette several times. His eyes! She had heard people tell of looking into someone's eyes and seeing insanity or evil; for the first time she understood. It was as if she had been looking into the eyes of a dead person who still stared at her and still moved.

Thoughts of the last few days stunned her. She found

herself almost believing that all of this – the capture, the terrifying Comanchero, the fiery inferno, the sudden escape – was a bizarre dream.

And this McLeod. *McLeod what?* she wondered. Was he just another Comanchero grabbing her for his own use? She looked back to the blue-and-yellow US Cavalry uniform pants and bitterness welled up inside her. She knew some Yankees weren't terrible people, but, when she saw blue uniforms, she could see or feel nothing except hatred. Images of the past overtook her.

Grady lay in the gray mud at Elmira Island, his one worn blanket now matted and pressed down into the wet mud. Tattered remnants of a gray Confederate overcoat with the epaulets of a colonel covered parts of his big body in a futile effort to relieve the chills that shook him. Dried blood from the officer who had once worn it still caked a quarter of the coat's surface. Grady was gaunt; his once powerful body now weighed little more than one half its usual two hundred pounds. Water lifted to his lips in a metal cup stank with the pollution of the prisoners' water supply. His face was the bright red of one consumed with massive infection.

Carlotta shook her head to rid herself of the images. She'd not seen Grady in prison, but it must have been like that. She tried to fight the bile back down. At least she was away from the Comanches and that Comanchero. But why was this McLeod here in the middle of Comancheria unless he was also some kind of a renegade, a Yankee renegade?

She dropped her hands to the rifle in the scabbard on

her saddle. From the stock of the rifle she knew it was a Spencer repeating rifle like the one her father carried. In her mind she reviewed the mechanism and mentally rehearsed getting it unsheathed and into action. Had this McLeod thought of the Spencer? Should she take it into her hands now before he had a chance to seize it?

When they crossed another small trickle of a stream, McLeod reined in his big buckskin, walked it away, and then turned back to face the way they had come. Carlotta pulled her horse up and watched him carefully. Even after she dismounted, she kept the horse positioned so that she could quickly get the Spencer into action.

He let his horse drink but watched in the direction from which they had come for a long time before he dismounted. Before he drank he emptied his canteen, filled it with fresh water and looked to see that she was doing the same with the Comanchero's leather water bag.

As he had bent to the little stream, his battered Stetson slipped from his head, held only by its chin strap.

Carlotta gasped audibly before she could clamp her hand across her mouth to stop herself. McLeod quickly snapped his hat back on to his head.

'Comanches?' she asked after an awkward moment. These were the first words either had spoken during the entire episode other than the brief exchange of names, she realized.

'Yankee artillery shell,' he replied. 'A fragment ripped my scalp off. Quicker than a Comanche but rougher.'

She pointed to the yellow-legged pants. 'Why those pants if the Yankees were shooting at you?'

McLeod kneeled, removed his hat and again revealed the hand-sized mass of rough scar tissue on the top of his head. He poured a hat full of the clay-stained water over his head, slung his head hard enough to rid himself of most of the water, brushed his remaining hair back into place with his hand and replaced the battered hat. His voice sounded easier to Carlotta than it had in their earlier, strained exchange of names.

'I nearly died in a Yankee prison,' he began slowly. 'Rather than die, I volunteered to fight Indians. "Galvanized Yankees" they called us. Yankee blue over Rebel gray.'

Carlotta turned stiffly away as bile roiled up inside her. She swung on to the bay and slammed her heels into its sides without turning her eyes back toward him.

'Well hello, Texas,' she heard him mutter. 'Guess you would have rather been with the Comanches.'

McLeod caught up and rode beside her without speaking again. Their pace was now slowed to a trot, mile eating but much less demanding on the horses. Carlotta was well aware of the problem of trying to save them and yet also try to gain precious miles on the Comanches; she couldn't fault him on his handling of the horses. They stopped again to water the horses at what Carlotta figured must be the Prairie Dog Town Fork of the Red River, about two miles below where it emerged from Palo Duro Canyon. Each avoided the other's eyes. From a quarter of a mile to the south, a pair of pronghorn antelopes watched them curiously. A dust devil whirled northward along the top of the Cap Rock. After watering the horses and then themselves, but not speaking, Carlotta and McLeod rode in the direction of the Texas settlements to the south-east.

After a few minutes, McLeod stopped on the middle of

a large stretch of bare stone. Carlotta whirled her horse and grabbed for the action of the Spencer rifle.

'Get off here,' he said without looking at her.

'Why?' she asked suspiciously, keeping her hand on the Spencer. Options flitted through her mind. If he moved toward her, she would ride him down then turn to shoot him.

McLeod didn't answer her question. Instead he pulled a sheet of buckskin from his over-sized saddle-bags and started cutting it into large patches. Carlotta didn't budge until he tossed her a large piece of the buckskin. She caught it with her left hand, hesitated, and then dismounted, careful to keep her horse between them and the Spencer rifle close to her right hand.

'Cut pieces large enough to cover each hoof and be tied four inches up the leg. Cut some for the mules too,' he directed her in a flat voice.

The resistance she always felt when men ordered her about flared, but she smothered the feeling and dug into the Comanchero's saddle-bags. She had never seen a man's belongings arranged in such neat and orderly fashion. She found a razor-sharp knife and began to work. By the time she had cut enough leather for the mules' feet, McLeod had tied the improvised boots on the horses and was waiting to do the pack mules, which had just caught up to them.

'Be interesting to see what's in those packs when we have time,' McLeod said without looking up at Carlotta.

She looked at the packs with new interest but said nothing. Instead she kept her attention on McLeod, mentally rehearsing how she would draw the Spencer and fire into the middle of his massive body if he tried to take control of her.

McLeod stood and faced her as he took the leather for the last mule. 'You not going to talk to me all the way back home?' he asked.

'My husband was captured, too. He died in a Yankee prison rather than wear those,' she hissed and pointed at McLeod's blue-and-yellow army pants as if her fingers were daggers.

'Every man had to make his own decision,' McLeod answered quietly and went back to booting the last mule.

'Grady chose not to become a traitor.'

McLeod ignored her and worked at booting the mules. The muscles along her jaw stood out more rigidly. Her lips pressed together, white at the edges.

When McLeod finished the last animal and mounted, he spoke without looking at her. 'This won't fool them for good, but it might buy us a little time.' He turned his horse back toward the Prairie Dog Town Fork, the opposite direction from the settlements.

'Why are we going this way?' Carlotta asked with suspicion in her voice.

McLeod paused but didn't look back toward her. 'The Comanches have that herd of captured horses. With their fresh horses, we'll kill ours if we try to outrun them. We can't outfight them, and it's unlikely we'll surprise them again.'

The truth of what he said was obvious to her, but she still wasn't ready to trust this traitor. She tossed her head to clear her raven curls out of her face. 'Where are we going in this direction?' she asked.

McLeod pointed toward the north-west. 'The Staked Plains. If lucky, on to Fort Sumner in New Mexico.'

Carlotta's eyes and mouth flew open in shock. 'You're crazy!'

'Crazy enough that you're not back with your old friends,' he said and pointed his head back the way they had fled the Comanches.

Carlotta stared dumbly at him. She couldn't believe this man was serious. Only a Comanchero would go up on to the Staked Plains. But still, this McLeod hadn't tried yet to disarm her.

McLeod shrugged his shoulders. 'Go whichever way you please.'

'Even Rangers won't go on to the Staked Plains,' she finally managed.

'I'd rather take a chance to live than die for sure,' he told her. The big man's eyes held hers for a long moment. Carlotta stared back without changing her hostile expression or speaking. McLeod shrugged slightly and spurred his horse away from her down a long ground-level rock runway toward the Prairie Dog Town Fork.

Carlotta sat motionless for at least a minute. Part of her wanted to flee toward home, but everything this man said rang true.

'You got the mules?' McLeod asked when she rode up behind him.

'Yes.'

'Keep to the rock until we're in the water,' he told her. 'If we don't leave any sign, we might gain several hours' lead.'

'Will that be enough?' she asked.

'It'll have to be,' he answered and rode toward the Staked Plains.

TWO

Ian Richards breathed deeply, clenched his fists more tightly than ever, exhaled slowly and took in the sweep of the landscape beyond the canyon. His harsh abuse of women had caused him to be driven away from more than one place, but out on the Staked Plains no one cared. He glanced around at his companions as if noticing them for the first time. These Comanches would kill him as quickly and thoughtlessly as they would a mosquito which disturbed their sleep, he knew. He took another deep breath and tried to compose himself.

Thundercloud, the leader of the raiding party, sat impassively, showing no emotion despite the anger he felt over losing a Tejano captive. He remained outwardly impassive in the face of Ian Richards's wrath as the other warriors sorted through supplies scorched by the fire the white man had sent among them. He silently reminded himself that he tolerated the Comanchero because he furnished badly needed goods from the New Mexico settlements. Without the Comanchero's trade, The People would be unable to purchase firearms, ammunition and iron products.

Ian Richards paced back and forth through the charred roots of grass, clenching and unclenching his talon-like fingers, although he knew that Comanches considered displaying such emotion to be a sign of weakness and thus sufficient reason to kill an outsider. He couldn't compose himself to speak in a more respectful tone to Thundercloud even though he knew the danger of his disrespect. His thin lips, made to look even thinner by his pencil-thin, black mustache, twisted as he raged. 'If we don't leave soon we may not catch the woman and the stranger,' he reminded Thundercloud for the third time.

Thundercloud had heard this strained, almost whispering tone of voice before when the Comanchero was excited about a woman. The Comanche leader looked away from Ian Richards and took a deep draught of smoke from a cigar taken on the raid in Texas, ignoring the Comanchero for a long moment.

'We have the horses,' Thundercloud finally responded. 'We will rest on the Llano.'

Ian Richards stopped pacing and stood over Thundercloud. 'You forget, Thundercloud. My pack mules are with them.'

A casual flip of Thundercloud's hand indicated his lack of concern.

'On the mules,' Richards continued in a calmer, stronger voice, 'are twenty-four rifles – new Henry repeaters.'

The veteran trader Thundercloud didn't change his expression but his stomach churned.

'Twenty-four Henrys would make you an even bigger man among the Quahidi Band,' Ian Richards added. He

17

knew how badly Thundercloud wanted to lead warriors on raids to Texas.

Thundercloud's complaisance melted. He began gathering his few items that had been left unburned. No words were necessary. At once the eleven remaining warriors began preparations to leave. Within ten minutes they were following the trail of the Tejano woman, her rescuer and the mules.

THREE

To Quentin McLeod, the wide maw of Palo Duro Canyon seemed as awesome as the gates of hell. Yet he found the canyon grippingly beautiful despite its reputation as the most important stronghold of the Comanches and a place even the boldest Texans considered sure death. Green cedars, junipers, bois d'arc and mesquite contrasted with the red soil, the bands of yellow and purple minerals in the canyon walls and the deep blue of the autumn Texas sky. Why, Quentin McLeod wondered, did the world always seem to look most beautiful when he was likely to be killed? It gave him the uncomfortable feeling that the world was getting ready to bid him goodbye.

McLeod halted his buckskin in the deep shadow of a cottonwood tree a couple of miles into the canyon. A quarter of a mile away a group of whitetail deer stood motionless watching the intruders, before they began to browse peacefully. A covey of quail scurried off, running like race horses away from the human interlopers. A honeybee buzzed by McLeod and Carlotta. The sun was now overhead, its warmth making it feel as if winter was much further away than it actually was. McLeod heard no sound other than the brisk breeze rustling the dry and yellowing cottonwood leaves nor smelled anything other than juniper and the sweat on the horses.

Carlotta rode up beside McLeod, careful not to let her horse step outside the water and leave sign that wouldn't wash away.

McLeod's eyes continued to scan the horizon as he greeted her. 'We can hide out, wait till dark and travel at night, or we can travel on and make miles from your bunch. Which do you think?'

His question surprised Carlotta. She seldom hesitated to express her opinions to men, but they rarely asked. She took a full minute to think before answering, although she had been considering the same alternatives ever since entering the canyon.

McLeod noted how effortlessly she handled the spirited bay captured from the Comanchero and admired the additional hue her blue dress added to the montage of the shrubs and canyon walls. He pushed his hat back and enjoyed the cool breeze against his bared head.

'We'd be less likely to run into other Indians at night,' Carlotta finally answered.

'True,' he responded, then remained silent for what seemed a long time while he watched the area of thick cedar and cottonwoods where the creek turned around a massive gray rock about a quarter of a mile ahead of them. Finally he turned his eyes to her and continued, ' 'Course your bunch may catch us if we lay up for very long.' It was the first time his speech had been comfortable with this woman.

Carlotta breathed deeply in relief. If McLeod was giving her a voice in deciding what to do, he must not be just another Comanchero taking her on to the Plains for his own use or to trade. Her mind returned to his question.

'You seem to have more experience with Indians,' she said. 'I'd take my chances riding on for a few more hours, but I'll follow your lead.'

When they came to the gray boulder, McLeod stopped and listened, unsure what made him uneasy. He saw nothing, heard nothing and smelled nothing unusual. His horse wasn't behaving suspiciously. He glanced at Carlotta's horse and the mules, but they didn't seem to find anything alarming. Finally, he rode ahead despite his apprehension.

Without knowing why he did so, McLeod swung his body back to his right just in time to see a brown blur hurtling down from a cedar-shrouded ledge. He kicked his feet free from his stirrups and managed to catch the attacker by both arms. He landed with a sickening thud and fought as maddeningly to get air back into his lungs as he did to keep the knife, only inches away, from slicing his throat. The warrior's braids flopped back and forth across his face. Animal fat smeared on the Comanche's skin made it harder and harder for McLeod, powerful though he was, to hold the wrist and keep the knife from his flesh.

McLeod's horse bucked and whirled away from the wild struggle going on beneath it; one of its hoofs caught the warrior in the back of the head and knocked him away from McLeod. Immediately McLeod sprang to his feet and dived on to the Comanche, trying to smash his knee into the warrior's crotch. The Comanche was quick enough to save his manhood; a sharp edge of shale slashed McLeod's knee.

Another Comanche appeared by the stream, hesitated for a moment, then pulled a war club from his belt and started forward. A loop settled over his head and tightened around his neck. The warrior paused in surprise, and whirled. The riata jerked him backwards.

The stocky Comanche recovered his balance, turned toward Carlotta and gathered himself to spring. Her eyes flared in alarm. Feelings and images flashed through her mind – her scalped mother, a warrior shaking blood from her own mother's scalp on her, an arrow sticking all the way through her father, the despair she had felt as her captors swept her further and further away from home.

'Back!' she snapped to her horse. As the warrior sprang, her horse scrambled backwards and snapped the line taut again. The Comanche tried to regain his balance, then stumbled forward; his neck caught in the prong formed by two limbs of a mesquite. Before he could recover his balance, the bay pulled the rope even tighter, snugging the warrior's neck to the limbs. He grasped the thick mesquite limbs; he strained desperately to gain slack, but the horse kept the slack out like he would a calf trying to get away. The warrior slowly sagged. His hands turned loose.

McLeod and his opponent warily circled each other with drawn knives, feinting but not committing to an attack. Suddenly McLeod felt as if a dozen hot coals were being stuck to his neck and face. Both combatants swiped free hands at the moving cloud of hornets whose nest had been dislodged by the horse's kicks.

McLeod reacted first. Already crouched, he threw himself backwards into the deepest part of the hole the creek had washed out as it swirled around the massive boulder. As he plunged underwater, he caught his feet on a rock ledge and gave a powerful thrust, propelling himself across the pool. For a brief moment the white ceiling of water shut McLeod off from the Comanche and the rest of the world, but then the water parted as the Comanche sliced face first through that ceiling.

As McLeod struggled to get his feet underneath himself, he saw a flash of a knife and felt a fiery sensation on his forehead. Once he was on his feet and the water was out of his eyes, blood poured down his face and partially blinded him. A few wet hornets remained. Several others still flew around and attacked again.

As the Comanche burst from under the water, McLeod recovered his balance enough to land a left hook that gashed the Comanche's cheek. Blood spattered. Without a pause McLeod followed with an overhand right, clubbing the Comanche with the butt of his knife. As he surged forward to follow up, a backhanded swipe from the warrior's knife barely caught his chest and left a new streak of blood. McLeod lost his knife.

Desperately he grabbed at the Comanche's right wrist and yanked it out of the way as he drove his head forward and crushed the Comanche's mouth and audibly shattered teeth. But it also left McLeod with a new ragged wound across his forehead. The momentum took both out of the pool.

The Comanche sagged visibly. It was win now or die. McLeod slammed his right fist as hard as possible into the warrior's groin. The warrior convulsed in pain. He grabbed the warrior's scrotum and ripped downward, lifted the warrior, slammed his shoulder into his midriff and drove him backwards into the sharp edge of a broken boulder.

The warrior gasped loudly. McLeod released the warrior and smashed upward with joined fists. The Comanche's head snapped back; his eyes dulled. With all the strength he had left, McLeod slammed the heel of his palm into the tip of the warrior's nose. The bridge of the nose collapsed and disappeared into the rest of the face. Blood gushed.

McLeod sagged to the ground, exhausted, gasping air into his burning lungs. The cuts and hornet stings felt like dozens of points of fire touching his skin. He tasted and smelled his own blood.

Carlotta's voice snapped him back alert. 'You think these were the only two?'

Two? He snapped his eyes to Carlotta. She sat in the saddle, her rope taut from the saddle horn to the head of the other Comanche whose neck was still caught in the mesquite. Carlotta's horse kept tension on the rope as he would a roped steer. Carlotta sat rigidly straight, her face pasty, her breath rasping in rapid, shallow draughts.

It took what seemed to him an enormous time for the scene to register. He quickly swept his eyes from horizon to horizon. At last he turned back to Carlotta. 'You can turn him loose now,' he told her, his voice slurred by exhaustion.

Carlotta eased her horse forward for a couple of steps, slid down and leaned with her face against her saddle. Her shoulders began to shake, then drooped. She turned and began to retch. McLeod caught her as she collapsed, attempted to support her. Instead, both sagged to the ground, arms around each other. Carlotta's sobbing surprised him. His exhausted mind couldn't pair her sobbing with the woman he'd seen spit in the

Comanchero's face and had so calmly waited in place for him to ride out of the flames and cut her loose. But he was too tired to contemplate that, so he concentrated on the present. At first McLeod held her very awkwardly and uncomfortably, then began to stroke her hair gently as if soothing a child.

Carlotta shook and clung more tightly. When he tried to release himself from her arms to move the horse, Carlotta clutched more desperately. McLeod held her against his chest, stroking the raven hair he thought so beautiful. He found himself liking her presence there against him more than he expected or wanted. After what seemed a long time, he sensed Carlotta steeling herself and drying her tears. When her grip loosened, he stood and carefully moved the horse.

His bruises and cuts hurt badly, and she must be in similar condition, he realized.

'We have to risk a fire,' she said and started to rise.

'Wait. Stay where you are for a minute.' McLeod sat back down and pulled off his boots. 'Give me your shoes.'

He removed the moccasins from the dead warriors, measured the two pairs against each other, and handed Carlotta the smaller.

Carlotta looked at the moccasins he handed her and burst out laughing. At McLeod's puzzled expression, she held the moccasin against her bare foot, which was at least two inches longer than the moccasin.

'You laugh pretty,' McLeod told her and tried to smile. He wanted to tell her how much he admired someone who could laugh during hard times, but the words wouldn't come. He switched moccasins with her and chuckled at her surprise when the smaller ones fit him.

His small feet at the bottom of his trunk-like legs looked odd to most people. Friends had often accused him of walking around on stumps.

'You have any coffee?' Carlotta asked.

She washed his wounds with warm water as he finished explaining his plan. 'Best we can hope for is to delay them again. Maybe we can make them think for a while that we were captured or killed.' He paused, enjoying the balm of warm water on sore muscles. He enjoyed her nearness in silence for a moment, then continued, 'They might relax and slow down a little. Every minute we gain gives us a better chance.'

Carlotta picked up one of her shoes and rubbed it in the blood still oozing from the slash across his chest. 'I'll leave this for them to find somewhere down the trail.'

McLeod nodded and winced as she washed out the chest wound again. A few minutes later, they were astride the Indian ponies and leading their horses with the dead Comanches tied across the saddles. A mile up the canyon Carlotta dropped her bloodied shoe. McLeod fished one of his dark cigars out of his saddle-bag. He lit it, enjoyed a deep drag off the strong tobacco, blew out the match and carefully stuck it into what remained of his shirt pocket. *I like this country!* McLeod thought to himself.

FOUR

The hat-sized fire used to cook a hot meal and make coffee had been extinguished. Heavy clouds blocked the light of the moon and stars. An already dark night became soot-black in the narrow side canyon off Palo Duro, a half day's ride from the confrontation with the two Comanches. The evening seemed unnaturally quiet. No scurrying animals could be heard; not a single coyote had yipped or howled. The smell of smoke from the smothered fire hung heavily around the camp.

McLeod stretched and tried to work out some of the soreness from the hard day and the battle with the Comanche warrior, then ran his hand across his face and across his rough beard. His fingers registered the lumps from the hornet stings, a large knot from his fall off the horse and the cuts from the Comanche warrior's knife and teeth. His forehead felt much like his scalp had felt after catching a Union artillery shard at the Battle of Chickamauga. He hurt from head to toe.

Carlotta leaned against a rock and stretched her long back and legs. As she ran her fingers down the blue dress, straightening the fabric, she could feel several small tears and rips in the sturdy linsey-woolsey material. With long fingers she swept her hair out of her face. She found it hard to believe that it was little more than eighteen hours since she had been tied to a mesquite stump and almost traded to a Comanchero. It seemed months rather than four days since the Comanches had captured her. The memories seemed like nightmares, terrible but not real. For once she was grateful for her life of farm and ranch work, sure that most of the softer girls from the towns wouldn't have survived the ordeal of captivity and runaway flight. McLeod and the canyon faded away. Her memory drifted back to her home. Time faded away from her as she played back through her mind the death of her parents, her capture and her wild ride to where she had been rescued by McLeod.

She could barely detect McLeod's shape in the darkness. She tried to think if he had been talking. Her mind raced back over the events since his appearance at the waterhole. The discovery of the two dozen Henry repeating rifles in the Comanchero's packs still shocked Quentin McLeod and Carlotta Mainord. She spoke as much to herself as to McLeod. 'It's not just the rifles. There's enough ammunition there to wipe out dozens of homesteads down home.'

The sudden flare of the match that Quentin struck to light a dark cigar reflected off the white strips from Carlotta's petticoat that now bandaged his chest, head, and knee. 'The rifles mean they can't let us get away,' he responded as the match burned out.

Both fell into a long silence. A red glow dimly illuminated McLeod's face as he inhaled on his cigar. The odor of tobacco smoke brought images of home to Carlotta, family gathered in front of a fireplace, a table filled with good things to eat, Carlotta's mother leaning toward the fire for better light by which to sew, Rebecca copying letters on to her black school slate. She swallowed to relieve the tightness in her throat as the images changed to her mother and her father stripped of clothing and scalped in the yard of their homestead. She quietly wiped her moist eyes, thankful for the darkness that hid her face.

McLeod's voice intruded into her memories and brought her back to the present. 'What's your last name?'

The question startled Carlotta. So much had happened, and they didn't really know each other's names. 'Mainord. Carlotta Mainord,' she answered. Carlotta wondered if he would seek no more knowledge. Eventually she took the initiative. 'What's your other name?'

'Quentin,' he answered. His voice had a southern drawl but also the hint of some other accent that Carlotta couldn't quite place. 'Quentin McLeod.'

'From Texas?' she asked after McLeod failed to elaborate or carry the conversation further.

'Florida. Euchee Valley, Florida,' he responded after another pause. 'That's on the Choctawhatchee River, up in the north-west part of the state.'

In the inky darkness, Carlotta's voice seemed to drift in from nowhere. 'You been back there since the war?'

McLeod stretched his legs, trying to find a comfortable position for his battered body before he answered. 'Once. There's nothing there for me, now.'

Carlotta's silence was so pronounced in the darkness that McLeod wished he could think of something to say. His mind raced, but he couldn't think of anything appropriate.

After several minutes, Carlotta finally broke the silence. 'Why did you do it?'

'What?' he asked.

'Switch sides,' she said, bitterness creeping into her voice despite her best efforts. 'Join the Yankees.'

Carlotta heard his knuckles pop as he clenched his fists. McLeod shifted position, extending his legs to the front and stretching his thick muscles. At last he spoke. 'I didn't even know she was expecting when I joined up. By the time I was in the Yankee prison, I had a three-year-old son I'd never seen. I was wounded and festering.'

For what seemed a long time, McLeod said nothing else, drawing heavily on the tobacco. Carlotta heard a stick snap, barely able to make out his big meaty hands breaking a juniper limb into small segments. About the time she decided he was going to say no more on the subject, he resumed. His voice seemed far away.

'My wife didn't want me to join up. We had no slaves . . . didn't want any. Most people in Walton County opposed secession. Delegates at the state secession convention took to calling us Lincoln County, because our delegates voted against secession over and over.'

He paused. Carlotta could see him lighting a new cigar from the old. The red glow reflected pink off the head bandage.

'Really, I just joined because everybody else did,' McLeod finally continued. 'I wanted to see the elephant – have one big adventure in my life. We were afraid the war was going to be over before we got into it.'

McLeod laughed lightly, without humor, as he remembered how naïve that had seemed later. Lightning

30

illuminated the sky and canyon. 'Seems a million years ago. We were all so young.'

'I wish Grady had done what you did,' Carlotta said. 'Grady was my husband.'

Carlotta fell silent, shocked at her words. She had never even thought such a thing, much less said it. Yet she realized that she meant it.

McLeod could feel her tension but didn't know what to say, not wanting to provoke the bitterness she had expressed earlier in the day, nor disrupt the ease with which they now talked. Finally Carlotta broke the heavy silence. 'What happened to your family? You said you had nothing to go home to.'

Like so many times before, his mind returned to the past.

He stood motionless, sodden from his brown hat to his US Army blue pants, staring at the graves. The soil was still bare, not enough time having passed to cover the raw dirt rectangles with grass. One of the rectangles was smaller than the other. He read the lettering again and again.

Jewel Mcleod
Born Isle of Skye, Scotland, April 21, 1837
Died Euchee Valley, Florida, April 21, 1866

Quentin McLeod
Born Euchee Valley, Florida, February 2, 1862
Died Euchee Valley, Florida, April 19, 1866

A steady stream of water ran off the front of McLeod's hat but didn't interfere with the reading of the tombstone inscriptions. It was as if the messages were etched into his soul.

'Cholera. I never saw the boy,' McLeod finally told Carlotta.

Flashes of light and a deafening roar yanked their thoughts away from the past and set the horses to bucking against their picket lines. Multiple bolts of lightning continued to strike. McLeod and Carlotta scrambled from the ground and raced to secure their stock. Huge, scattered drops of cold rain pelted them, turned to a downpour and quickly plastered their wet clothing to their bodies. The temperature dropped dramatically. Gusts of wind whipped the juniper shrubs as if they were blades of grass. The wind against their sodden clothing chilled both to the bone.

McLeod hunched his shoulders as he led the two mules to where Carlotta tried to quiet Buck and the bay, her teeth chattering so badly that McLeod could hear them over the wind. He shouted to be heard, although he was only a few feet away from Carlotta. 'We better get up higher toward the rim. Saddle our horses and I'll pack the mules.'

'If we go up on the flats, lightning may get us,' Carlotta replied as she worked with the horses, the task of fastening cinches made difficult by the numbness in her fingers.

McLeod leaned toward Carlotta and shouted again to be heard. 'What?'

'Lightning may get us up there,' she yelled.

He leaned even closer to her and shouted, 'If we stay here, we may drown.'

Carlotta had seen enough Texas storms to know he was right. She felt something against her back and shoulders and flinched before she realized it was McLeod trying to get her into his leather coat. The leather felt sodden and cold, but she pulled it as tightly around herself as she could. Despite the sodden feel of the leather, the coat made her feel there was some protection between her and the driving rain. She wrapped her arms around herself and tried to feel free of the elements, then pushed her hands out and began to tighten saddles on the horses.

Ten minutes later Carlotta and McLeod rode up the side canyon. Behind them the two dead Comanches from their morning encounter had been left covered by a caved in bank of dirt. McLeod and Carlotta hoped the coming rains would wipe out the sign of the burial as well as their own tracks. Lightning streaked eerily across the sky. Thunder roared like a big artillery battle of the late war.

Neither Carlotta nor McLeod said anything as a new roar drowned out the thunder. Both spurred their horses up a steep slope that they could only hope would lead them all the way to the top of the cap rock.

The horses scrambled desperately, their hoofs slipping, their bodies convulsing in panicked effort. Before they could make half a dozen jumps, a solid wall of water roared around the bend of the canyon.

They drove their terrified animals even harder. Buck grunted loudly enough to be heard over the storm, squealed in fear and effort. Constant lightning kept the deadly surge of storm water visible. The mules screamed and drove past Carlotta and McLeod, their surer footing making the work easier. Without thinking, Carlotta grabbed desperately at the tail of the nearest mule as it passed by. Her fingers grasped the coarse hair momentarily before it slipped away.

McLeod reined Buck in and used his reins to slash Carlotta's faltering bay across the haunches. The long-legged bay's eyes rolled, and its head flounced as it scrambled desperately up the last steep stretch of canyon wall. Its feet slipped; it slid backwards. McLeod whacked the bay again and it responded with one last frantic lunge. It fell to its knees then fought back on to its feet on the Cap Rock of the Staked Plains.

McLeod lay forward to help his horse, now up to its haunches in the raging current. Continuous flashes of lightning illuminated the scene as brightly as daytime, but in a much eerier light. Thus McLeod received his first sight of the Staked Plains stretching away in the torrential rainfall. The long grass lay against the ground in the wind, looking like a water-slicked rug. Sheets of water already ran off the Cap Rock into the canyon. Then the light disappeared as quickly and completely as when a candle is snuffed out.

A rope loop settled around the buckskin's neck. Another flash of light revealed Carlotta and her bay at the edge of the Cap Rock, the taut rope from Buck's neck to the horn of Carlotta's saddle. The bay squatted on its haunches his feet plunging like pistons as he tried to pull McLeod's buckskin over the last ledge and on to the Cap Rock of the Staked Plains. The bay skidded toward the edge of the canyon, then caught its footing again and surged forward.

The extra pull from the rope and its own lunge got the buckskin's front feet on to the top. McLeod vaulted from the saddle and struggled to pull the big horse up by the reins. The rope from the other horse strained to the verge of breaking. Just as the lightning again cast its strange glow upon the scene, the buckskin popped above the rim like a cork from a champagne bottle.

Brilliant streaks of lightning turned the scary scene into daylight. Raging red water roiled within feet of the top of their canyon. Three hundred yards down, the current tossed the Indian ponies down the stream like corks.

The bizarre display of lightning struck the surface of the Staked Plains continuously at a dozen points at any one time. The two fugitives, their horses and the mules, were the highest objects for miles around. McLeod leaned toward Carlotta and cupped his hands against the noise. 'Welcome to the Staked Plains, Carlotta Mainord. Let's get a move on. If we're going to be lightning rods, let's at least make some miles and hope the rain lasts long enough to wash out the tracks.'

As they headed west, McLeod turned back to Carlotta once again and shouted to be heard over the rain, wind, and thunder. 'If this keeps up, we just might have a chance. Not much of one, but more chance than we had before.'

FIVE

Carlotta and McLeod chewed dried meat and drank from their canteens after a couple of hours of sleep. The rest, as well as the time spent riding the Comanches' ponies the previous day, had left their horses in relatively good shape, more than could be said for Carlotta and Quentin.

The peacefulness seemed particularly eerie in contrast to the previous day's violence, the near escape from the sudden flood and the terrifying experience of riding through the lightning storm. Shades of red, pink and lavender played off the remaining blotches of black clouds in the eastern sky. McLeod and Carlotta rested in a spot slightly higher than the surroundings on the Staked Plains, which, to the eye, stretched flat all the way to the horizon in every direction. Not a single tree or shrub broke the smooth line. The horses and mules grazed on the knee-deep grass. Carlotta pointed to the tall grass rippling in the breeze as far as the eye could see. 'Reminds me of waves on the Gulf.'

'I've heard that some of the Spanish conquistadors felt seasick watching it,' McLeod responded. 'Back home—'

'Someone's coming!' Carlotta interrupted.

McLeod followed her gaze and picked up the moving dots barely visible just above the southern horizon. He watched silently for some minutes, then picked up his bridle and headed to the horses.

Carlotta gathered their gear, moving quickly but calmly, while McLeod saddled the horses. In a couple of minutes, she joined McLeod and helped him pack the rifles and ammunition on to the mules. Both regularly checked the dots moving slowly and steadily toward them.

McLeod stopped and leaned across the saddle of his horse, cupped his hands around his eyes and stared into the distance. After a moment, he whistled softly. 'Buffalo. That's buffalo, not people. Look at them!'

Thousands of the shaggy beasts gradually emerged from the distance, casually grazing their way north. McLeod leaned his arms across his saddle, now relaxed. 'That's what I came looking for.'

'Why'd you come all the way to the edge of the Staked Plains looking for buffalo?' Carlotta queried, realizing how little she still knew about him.

He lifted his canteen from his saddle horn, took another strip of jerky from his saddle-bag and sat down to resume his chewing. He gestured toward the herd with his handful of jerky. Carlotta sat back down and reclined on the grass, as relaxed as if on a Sunday picnic.

'Quick money,' McLeod told her. 'I've hide-hunted in Nebraska and Kansas. No one's taken hides here . . . yet. I wondered if I could get in and get out before Comanches caught me.'

'Can you?' she asked.

'Nae,' McLeod answered with the Scottish burr slipping back into his voice as she had noticed it sometimes did.

'I'll be happy if we get out of here once.'

She looked him over carefully, as if seeing him for the first time. 'You like hide-hunting?'

He washed down the last bite of jerky and shook his head. 'I hate the killing and waste, but it's a chance to make money in a hurry.'

'The Yankees must have rubbed off on you,' Carlotta said and caught him checking her facial expression out of the corner of his eye. She tried to keep a straight face, but a hint of a mischievous smile sneaked on to her lips. She flipped her head back to get her hair out of her eyes and tried to appear serious.

McLeod laughed. He could be a handsome man if he were cleaned up, she decided. On second thought, she determined that perhaps she was exaggerating – not a bad-looking man if he cleaned up and kept his hat on.

At the moment he was awfully ragged both in clothing and body. The rough tear across his forehead from the Comanche's teeth and the knife slash across his chest were bandaged with the white strips from her petticoat. The fire that had covered their escape from the Comanches had raised blisters on his face and left hand, although rain had washed the smell of singed hair from him. Hornet stings had left swollen red welts around his face; his left eye was half shut. He'd torn his right pant leg open to bandage his gashed knee and his shirt had also fared badly.

He had suffered much more wear and tear than she, Carlotta thought. Mainly she felt dirty. Her nose wrinkled at her smell. 'You know what I want more than anything?' she asked, then almost chuckled at the sudden, concerned look on his face.

His brow furrowed. 'To be home?' he asked.

'Nae, laddie,' she answered, imitating his Scottish burr now that she had pinned down the accent.

His face relaxed. 'Hot coffee?'

'A bath,' she responded. 'You got a wash in the creek, yesterday.'

McLeod looked sharply at her. 'A wash? That wasn't a leisurely soak I had.'

'I wish I had taken a bath while we were beside the creek,' she insisted.

'You look good,' he told her seriously.

Carlotta flipped her hair back again. 'A man wouldn't understand,' she bantered. The pleasure his compliment gave surprised her.

'You have any kids?' McLeod asked.

'No,' she responded, surprised at the question. A familiar, empty feeling struck her again. She stopped just short of telling him it was none of his business, then took a breath and calmed herself. The discomfort was in her voice despite her effort to keep it out. 'Grady and I wanted children, but there never were any.'

McLeod tried to turn the conversation in another direction. 'The frontier can be a tough place for kids and parents.'

Carlotta gazed into the distance and avoided looking at McLeod. 'Grady had a child with Zadie, his first wife,' she recounted, her voice tense but controlled. 'They lived near Indianola on the coast. She and Andrew, their baby, died in a typhoid epidemic. She was expecting again when she died.'

McLeod shifted, unsure of how to respond.

'Apparently I'm not capable of having a child,' she added.

'Did that bother Grady?' McLeod asked softly.

'He always said that it didn't. Said there are always plenty of kids needing a home and family on the frontier. But he loved kids.'

The rim of the sun rose above the edge of the Staked Plains. A skunk walked into view in a spot bare of grass not far away. Carlotta scuffed her feet gently to let the skunk get away without feeling threatened and spraying. Grady had told her that several fellows with whom he had driven cattle were more afraid of being bitten by rabid skunks while sleeping on the ground than of bullets, arrows or stampedes. She had always been able to get along with skunks if she saw them early enough not to threaten them.

McLeod's voice drew her thoughts from the skunks back to the Staked Plains. 'What was he like?'

Carlotta sat silently for a long moment. She broke off a long blade of grass and poked at an ant with it. 'Grady was a big man, a good bit taller than you and almost as large. Lots of men were scared of him. He had the reputation of a bad man to make trouble with.'

'Did Grady scare you?'

Carlotta smiled slightly. 'Grady was really one of the kindest men I ever knew. He was never much for talking,' she added.

'Did that bother you?'

Carlotta pulled off one of the moccasins she was wearing and looked carefully at the stitching as if inspecting it. She remained silent as she remembered the long rides they had taken on the prairies. While Grady sometimes rode for hours without speaking, he could always find time to stop and admire blue bonnets and Indian paint brush, or watch colors change at sunset, or chuckle at a quail hen fluttering off and feigning a broken wing to lure away the threat to her chicks.

'He was a kind and thoughtful man,' she answered at last. 'That was more important.'

Carlotta eased the moccasin back on to her foot, lay back against the grass, and stretched her legs luxuriantly. She closed her eyes as her mind wandered far into the past, silent so long that McLeod turned his attention to arranging his saddle-bags and other gear. He retrieved his boots from his saddle where he had put them when they had put on moccasins. 'It's a wonder these are still here after last night,' he commented as he pulled them on.

McLeod's words didn't register with Carlotta. Tears streaked her face. After a moment her shoulders shook with sobs as she surrendered to her emotions. McLeod pulled her to him.

'Grady was gruff sometimes, and he didn't talk to me much, but I loved him. I hoped for a long time that the letter I had received was wrong; that he was really alive. Finally an ex-soldier from Lavaca County came to see me and tell me that the other Texans in the prison camp had given him a decent burial.'

McLeod hugged her more closely. Her body convulsed with great, tearing sobs. It was as if Grady had just died. She let herself go and no longer tried to hold back or control tears or sorrow. Suddenly she felt consumed by an uncontrollable fury. She pulled away from McLeod and began swinging her fists, slamming him hard three times before he managed to catch her arms and pin them to her side. She struggled fiercely to get free and hit this man, a witness to her weakness and a survivor. Angry words poured out, punctuated by attempts to punch and claw at

McLeod. 'Damn you! Grady could have done the same thing as you. He could have worn the blue. He'd probably be alive like you.'

Finally Carlotta quit trying to hit McLeod and began sobbing again, her fury replaced by a sense of loss. 'I wish he'd done what you did,' she said through tears. 'Maybe he would have come home, too.'

Carlotta sagged against McLeod and clutched her arms tightly around him as she sobbed. 'Damn your stubborn hide, Grady Mainord! Why didn't you save yourself and come home to me?'

She continued crying, but the fury was gone. After she stopped, McLeod loosened his grip, but Carlotta continued to lean on his shoulder drawing comfort from his solid mass.

'I'm sorry I opened the old wounds,' McLeod told her gently.

'I don't hate you because of what you did. I'm just sorry Grady didn't do the same thing,' she responded, fury back in her voice. 'I could spit in his eyes I'm so angry at him for not saving himself!'

She shocked herself with her words but realized their truth. She settled against McLeod's chest and rested there for a long time. There were occasional sniffles, but the anger and sadness dissipated with the tears that wet his shirt. After a long time Carlotta sat up, more relaxed and composed.

She smiled, her eyes still sparkling with moisture. 'I won't hit you any more.'

'Truth is, men were probably afraid of Grady because he was married to you,' McLeod teased gently. 'Can't say as I blame them.' The two settled back into a comfortable silence. McLeod watched the herd intently for some time before he spoke. 'Those buffalo may be another lucky break for us.'

SIX

Bitter disappointment gnawed at Thundercloud as the Comanches rode up on to the Staked Plains in the dull light of dawn. Their quarry had been so near until the storm covered the fugitives' escape. The memory of seeing them in the flashes of lightning, yet being unable to get to them, infuriated him again.

Now he was unsure about the direction the two had taken. They could have gone any direction and covered a considerable distance while the storm was washing out tracks. Thundercloud considered choices available to the two they sought. His grudging respect, begun by the discovery that the two had taken this path up on to the Llano Estacado, grew with their defeat of the two warriors of The People and their survival of the flood in Palo Duro Canyon. There would be great honor in killing them, but they were wily. A good trick at this point, Thundercloud knew, would be if the two doubled back into Palo Duro Canyon and hid out until the Comanches gave up the search. If they didn't move, they wouldn't leave sign. Or they could head north to the Canadian River brakes where they could either hide out or move toward Fort Sumner under the cover of the canyons. Thundercloud thought this the least likely option since it would make the journey to Fort Sumner days longer, but they had surprised him already.

At last Thundercloud dispersed the warriors on different routes. They would try to find some clue as to where their quarry had gone after their tracks disappeared.

The aroma of frying bacon and boiling coffee awoke McLeod to find Carlotta working over hot coals in a narrow trench. A strong breeze took the smoke of the cooking fire through a thick cover of plum trees, dispersing it before it rose over the walls of the narrow canyon along the brakes of the Canadian. The horses and mules grazed on a nearby patch of grass, almost springtime-green here in this protected, moist pocket. Beyond them a line of large rocks dislodged by the erosion of the last big rain had fallen off the canyon side and formed a natural dam that trapped a large pool of water. For a leisurely moment McLeod lay still, enjoying Carlotta's beauty and the smooth grace with which she moved, then he sat bolt upright. The shadows were on the wrong side of the canyon!

'Is it afternoon?' he asked.

Carlotta set a skillet with thick slices of bacon and two pieces of fresh skillet-bread beside him. A moment later she set a cup of steaming coffee beside it. He tried to think about the strange afternoon light and shadows being all wrong, but instead he was thinking about how much he liked having Carlotta nearby when he woke up.

'You're a good sleeper when you put your mind to it,

Scotsman,' she told him.

Did her voice really sound that happy, he wondered? Or was he simply hearing what he wanted to hear? He felt as if his stomach was stuck to his backbone. He blew across the top of his cup and took a big swallow then hunched forward and opened his mouth to suck in big draughts of air. 'Whew! That'll burn all the hair off my tongue,' he told her. 'Just the way I like it,' he quickly added.

'Grady always said coffee should be strong enough to float a horseshoe and hot enough to melt one.'

McLeod enjoyed looking up at Carlotta, appreciating her raven hair sharply outlined against the sky. Her eyes were an even deeper shade of blue than the West Texas autumn sky, he decided.

'Grady had good taste,' he responded after a moment. He was hit by the surprising realization that he had known Carlotta for no more than a day and a half, yet he felt so comfortable talking to her. He had never felt comfortable talking to a beautiful woman except for Jewel. Since Jewel's death, conversation with any woman had been rare, yet it seemed so natural and right for her to be here bantering with him.

Carlotta declined McLeod's offer of bacon from the skillet. 'Ate while I cooked. You rest easy and watch for Comanches while you eat.' She tossed a square of yellow lye soap into the air and caught it with her other hand. 'I found more than bacon in your pack.' She inclined her head playfully toward the mouth of the small side canyon and away from the pool. 'Like I said, eyes down canyon.'

It had been six years since McLeod left for the war. In all that time, no other woman had interested or moved him. Now he wanted to hold Carlotta against him, to. . . .

He tried to banish the thoughts. It was too soon to think serious thoughts, the circumstances all wrong.

He sat the skillet aside, stood and tried to stretch away the stiffness from the hours in the saddle, the brutal fight and then, finally, long hours of sleep.

'I hear someone moving around,' Carlotta called, her voice more playful than disturbed.

'I've been asleep for eighteen hours,' he told her. 'I'm headed the other direction.'

When McLeod returned, he could hear splashing on the other side of the rocks. 'You still there?' he asked.

'I may stay in here until dark,' she responded. Her voice sounded as if she were enjoying the finest luxury of a plush hotel, McLeod thought warmly. Then he had to snicker a bit at himself. What did he know of any plush hotel? Sounded like something he would read in a book.

McLeod settled back down on to his blanket and started wiping the bacon grease from the skillet with his fry bread. 'Good vittles!' he called out to Carlotta. He leaned back against his saddle to enjoy the food, the afternoon sky, and the good coffee at his leisure.

The last swab of bread and bacon grease stopped halfway to his mouth as three men materialized in front of him like ghosts. Each carried a rifle, two Henry repeaters and one Spencer carbine. The man in the middle wore a black eye patch over the left eye surrounded by a mass of dark scar tissue. All three were filthy and had scraggly beards. The two on either side looked Mexican, while the one in the middle was obviously an Anglo, so light-skinned that he looked almost like an albino. One look marked all three as hard cases. McLeod chewed the bread slowly and picked up his coffee. He took time to swallow and sip some coffee before he finally spoke. 'Coffee's hot, fellows. Join me.'

The man in the middle looked even more evil when he smiled, revealing rotting uneven teeth. 'You're a real gentleman to offer,' he said, obviously enjoying the situation. 'Yes, sir, a real gent,' he sneered. 'We'll take that coffee along with anything else we want.'

The other two men nervously skirted the area with their eyes. The nearest seemed the more anxious of the two and kept flipping his eyes back to the two saddles nearby. McLeod couldn't put his finger on the reason, but he figured this was the most dangerous one and the one he'd try to take out first when it came to shooting. 'Where's the other person?' the nervous one finally asked.

McLeod's mind raced. His rifle was three feet away leaning across his saddle, but the three strangers had their rifles in their hands, their eyes and rifle muzzles pointed directly toward him. If they asked about the other person, they must not have been watching for long. As hard as he thought, McLeod couldn't come up with any strategy that made sense.

'I'm the other person,' Carlotta announced and stepped into the open, holding her dress in front of her. The intruders' eyes riveted hungrily upon her. She allowed the dress to drop, revealing her full naked figure.

McLeod rolled quickly to his right, caught up his Henry, rolled once more and came up on one knee shooting. His first round caught the closest man, the anxious one, in his left armpit and slammed him backward into the way of the other two. His second shot hit the man in the middle in the upper neck tearing his throat away and spattering blood over the third man. Immediately

McLeod pumped another round into the first man who was raising his weapon again.

Suddenly, everything seemed to be happening in molasses-slow motion. McLeod's eyes shifted to the third man and found the Spencer's muzzle that looked as big as a cannon aimed at him. He frantically swung his rifle toward the man and braced for the round he knew was bound to hit him. He had to survive the round and take this last man out. A fist-sized gray rock bounced off the brigand's head just as the muzzle of the Spencer blasted fire. The bullet grazed McLeod's shoulder as the man's rifle jerked upward.

McLeod didn't miss. He quickly levered and fired a second shot into the man's chest. A quick look at the other two confirmed that all were dead.

Carlotta stood frozen in the background with another rock poised to throw, her face as fierce as that of any Indian warrior McLeod had ever seen.

'It's over,' McLeod told her, his voice strangely gentle after the brief orgy of violence.

Carlotta gradually lowered the rock, then rushed over and hugged him so hard it was as if she was trying to smother him. McLeod sensed his body responding to her nakedness. He pulled her even closer and stroked her back, enjoying how firm and smooth her curves felt to his callused hands.

Carlotta jerked back and looked at the blood on her hand. 'You're hit!'

'Not hard, I don't think,' he tried to assure her. At the moment he wasn't concerned about the wound. He felt warm from head to toe. He tried to keep his eyes on her face but had to glance down. She was magnificent.

Carlotta blushed all the way to her bare feet. 'Oh my God!' Quickly she covered herself with the blanket on which McLeod had slept and now half-heartedly offered to her. 'I forgot.' She blushed all over again and wrapped the blanket around herself. She turned back to the shallow groove the bullet had cut across McLeod's left shoulder.

'You saved us,' he told her. 'You distracted them so I could get off a shot.' He paused and grinned. 'Of course, I nearly forgot to shoot, too.'

Carlotta blushed once more. 'The Lord gave us all a few weapons. It's up to us to do the best we can with them.'

McLeod had never thought that he could feel for any woman other than Jewel what he was feeling. And after such a short time! He was ready to settle in the brakes of the Canadian River for a nice, long time. He wanted to hold her close, to. . . . But it was too soon. The circumstances. . . .

'I better make sure there aren't any others,' he told her and turned reluctantly away. He retrieved his Henry, reloaded, and made sure that there were extra cartridges in his coat pocket.

'Now don't go chucking rocks at me when I come back,' he told her and walked down the canyon.

McLeod winced as Carlotta washed his wound. Carlotta set the pot back on to the coals and began to wrap the shoulder with another strip of her rapidly disappearing petticoat. McLeod grimaced again as she gave a last, hard tug on the bandage. Carlotta put her arms around the big man and pulled him to her in a strong hug. 'Don't be a big baby.'

She released him and stood. McLeod admired her

smooth, fluid movements. 'I am a big baby. I could use another hug.'

'You could use a bath,' Carlotta parried playfully. 'Soap's on the other side of the rocks.'

SEVEN

Dark Wolf stared into space trying to decide the direction of the seven rapid rifle shots that had just faded into the distance. He had just found where the tracks of two shod horses and two mules emerged from the buffalo tracks and turned down into the canyons leading toward the river. From the tracks he could tell that the horses had riders and the mules were heavily loaded.

He weighed his choices. He could ride toward the shots and investigate, or he could get the rest of the war party to join him. The young warrior felt almost certain that these were the tracks of the man who had appeared from the fire and the Tejano woman he stole. Although Dark Wolf would like the glory of taking the man and woman himself, he also remembered Thundercloud's violent temper. He decided to scout the trail first, and, when sure that this was the trail of those he sought, decide whether or not to go after the pursued by himself. He gauged the distance of the sun above the horizon and decided to follow as far as possible in the short time before dark.

*

A column of smoke rose straight and high through the clear morning sky. When the dry wood burned down into a good bed of coals, Dark Wolf piled green brush from the canyon on to the fire. When this was burning well enough to form a thick column of dark smoke visible for miles, he covered and uncovered the fire every few seconds with his sleeping robe. The repeated puffs of dark smoke, in series of threes, could be seen for a great distance over the flat Llano Estacado. To the south, Ian Richards, Thundercloud and the five Comanche warriors who hadn't been sent westward to scout toward Fort Sumner, pushed their horses hard toward the signal.

In a side canyon east of the signal fire, McLeod and Carlotta watched the same smoke signal climb through the bright morning sky. Carlotta handed McLeod a cup of coffee, blew gently across hers and finally spoke what both silently speculated. 'Must have been close enough to hear the shots yesterday afternoon.'

McLeod sipped the coffee and nodded agreement. 'You think we should make a run for it or stick tight?' he asked.

Carlotta's father had always urged his children to take time, whenever possible, to think before making important decisions, so she hesitated before she responded. 'We have extra horses now from those three renegades, so we could switch horses every few miles and make a good run. . . .'

McLeod countered, 'If we take the rifles, the mules might slow us down. We could leave them here.'

'No!' Fire flashed in Carlotta's deep-blue eyes. 'No one else needs to go through what I have. The Comanches will get the rifles if we leave them.'

McLeod nodded his agreement. Carlotta sipped coffee, flipped her hair back and continued, 'If we stay put we'll leave no tracks.'

McLeod lit one of his small cigars with a stick from the small fire. He was soon going to be out of the smokes. He silently wondered whether rabbit tobacco like he had smoked as a boy in Florida also grew in the Texas Panhandle.

'They'll find our tracks where we came off the Cap Rock into the canyons,' he countered again. 'We could fort up here and make a stand.'

Carlotta flicked an ant off the bandage around his head. 'I think time would be on their side.'

'My thinking, too,' McLeod responded. He took her long fingers in his massive hand, kissed her fingertips, spoke again. 'No telling how many other Comanches they can bring in if they need.'

Carlotta had reached her conclusion. 'I think we should take our chances and make a run for it. If the mules slow us down, we can let them go. They might take the rifles and leave us alone.'

'Do you believe that?' he asked, as he gently squeezed her hand and released it.

'No,' she answered immediately.

McLeod picked up a saddle and headed for the horses. Carlotta began packing their supplies. Both worked quickly. 'Glad we got a couple of good nights of sleep,' McLeod told her as he made a diamond hitch to lash a case of rifles to one of the mule's pack saddles.

'And my bath,' Carlotta answered without breaking the rhythm of her packing.

Two hours later Carlotta and McLeod paused in a thick

stand of cottonwood and sycamore trees west of the spot where they had first entered the brakes of the Canadian. McLeod thought he had never seen fall colors more beautiful than the bright yellow of the cottonwoods and coppery brown of the sycamores against the deep blue of the West Texas sky. A whitetail doe bolted from the trees and raced gracefully down the canyon to the river. McLeod pointed out the deer to Carlotta. If they were likely to die at any hour, he didn't want them to miss any of the beauty of this world.

Carlotta reached over and caught McLeod's arm. 'I smell smoke.'

They sat silent and motionless for several minutes before crossing an open space into a thick copse of plum and cedar in the upper reaches of a side. Large rough blocks of stone littered the ground. Layers of red, yellow and orange minerals streaked the bare soil of the canyon walls. Afternoon shadows were beginning to lengthen as tall cotton-white clouds drifted overhead.

'Wait for me,' he told her as he untied his jacket from behind his saddle, shrugged into it and checked its big side pockets for extra cartridges. He started to walk away but stopped and turned back toward Carlotta. She slid down from her horse and stood expectantly.

McLeod returned and laid his hand on Carlotta's hip. 'You're quite a woman, Carlotta Mainord. Beautiful, too.'

Carlotta flipped her head back to get the hair out of her eyes and smiled in a way that warmed McLeod all the way through. 'When we get to Fort Sumner, get some new pants. Okay, cowboy?'

McLeod leaned forward, took her in his arms and kissed her gently. She kissed back harder and squeezed him tightly. For a moment she clung, then pushed herself back away. 'Make sure you come back to get me, you hear?'

The last thing in the world that Quentin McLeod wanted at that moment was to take his arms from around Carlotta Mainord and go looking for what might turn out to be a hard death. But he had to.

McLeod slipped through the brush toward a rough tongue of rock that extended off the Cap Rock above and in front of them. He no longer had life plans that didn't include Carlotta, but for the moment he had to clear her from his mind and concentrate on whatever lay ahead. Short of the crest he dropped to his hands and knees and eased his eyes above the edge, taking care to break his outline in a growth of tall grass. A young warrior sat on a stony outcropping about twenty feet away.

McLeod quickly reached a decision. He took time to look carefully for any twig that might snap, any rock that might roll. The last thing they needed were rifle shots to speed more Comanches to the scene.

Dark Wolf emerged from the reverie and looked around. The fire was now a bed of coals. The smoke had died down. Although he knew better, he slipped back into his daydreaming and thought of the white woman they were pursuing.

Moments later, although he saw no one, he could feel that someone was nearby. He whirled and found the man who had ridden from the fire and seized the woman standing within an arm's length. Before he could move, the Tejano's rifle butt swept toward his face. Pain exploded in his face. The world went dark. McLeod followed up and drove the heel of his rifle butt between Dark Wolf's eyes.

Carlotta dismounted and knelt by the young Comanche's body. 'He is called Dark Wolf,' she told McLeod. 'He fed me when I was a prisoner and spoke to me in Spanish . . . he's so young.'

'Our good luck,' McLeod responded. 'I'd never have been able to sneak up on one of the older warriors.'

Carlotta lingered over the body of Dark Wolf; her fingers gently traced the young chin. 'He tried to help me when another, Red Bull, would have . . . hurt me.'

McLeod rolled Dark Wolf over so that Carlotta wouldn't have to look at his face. He put his arm lightly around her shoulders as he stood surveying the surroundings. 'You ever play poker?' he asked.

'Many a night,' she responded. 'My dad, mother, brothers, Rebecca and I would play. Later Grady, too. We had colored rocks for chips. Sometimes we didn't see another soul for weeks. Poker, tall tales, singing . . . seems years ago now.'

McLeod had been half listening, but now he turned and looked her directly in the eyes. 'What do you think about anteing up for the big pot right here?'

'You mean fort up here?' she asked, looking around at the canyon.

'More like a trap,' he told her.

'I'm game,' she said.

'You're the bait.'

EIGHT

The warriors sat on the edge of the Cap Rock and looked down into the pocket where Dark Wolf tended his fire, surprised to see the packed mules and the horses of the two they pursued. On the ground nearby lay the bodies of the woman and the Tejano. Blood covered the woman's head above the blue dress; her scalp was missing. A blanket covered the Tejano's head.

'This is why Dark Wolf is so excited,' Two Dog told Thundercloud and smiled his approval. 'It is a great coup for such a young warrior.'

Below, the warrior stood over the fire, his body wrapped in a blanket and his back turned toward the arriving party.

'Dark Wolf can be calm now. He plays the part well,' Two Dog told Thundercloud, chuckling.

Thundercloud whistled like a quail. The warrior waved in such a way that it was obvious that he wasn't surprised at their presence. Thundercloud was even more amused to see that Dark Wolf had painted his face red and black, more common among their northern neighbors than among The People.

Ian Richards cursed loudly, livid that the woman had

been killed. He had thought of little other than making this sassy woman bleed and cower.

When the Comanches rode on to the canyon bottom, near the fire, the warrior turned and dropped the blanket. The warriors were stunned to see full female breasts. During the moment that the warriors sat motionless from surprise, Carlotta raised a Henry and fired almost point blank into the belly of the nearest Comanche. A grim smile split her painted face.

On the other side of the fire, McLeod rose from beneath the blanket and fired into the shocked warriors. Two saddles emptied. Wild war cries filled the air. The other four warriors leaped their horses toward Carlotta.

Carlotta shot the first horse in the chest. It gave one loud grunt and crumpled, its hoofs slinging dirt on to her. Carlotta stepped to the side and pumped two shots into the downed warrior, firing so quickly that the two shots sounded like one. McLeod desperately tried to get his rifle lined on to a warrior. His first shot missed, but the second cut across another warrior's abdominal muscles, spilling his intestines and blood into the dust. The old warrior rolled when he hit the ground then managed to sit.

Another warrior leaped his horse across a downed comrade and slammed a war club into the back of Carlotta's head. She collapsed; blood pooled immediately. McLeod rushed desperately toward her and levered three quick shots at the warrior as he yelled triumphantly and raised his club to the sky. His third shot tore away the top of the warrior's head.

Thundercloud screamed the fierce war cry that had struck fear into so many enemies over the last thirty years and leaped his black stallion forward. McLeod whirled, pumped three rounds into the horse's chest, and leveled his rifle at the war chief's chest.

A hammer-like blow drove McLeod backward to the ground. Across the little valley, Ian Richards lowered the old Hawken rifle he had picked up from one of the Comanches and rode toward the mules.

Blood poured from McLeod's chest below his left shoulder, but his head remained clear. He had to act before the shock from the wound took full effect.

Thundercloud struggled from underneath his horse and advanced carefully, unsteady on his feet, his knife in his hand. Without thinking, McLeod pulled the Colt from his holster and fired from the hip. Thundercloud spun to the ground.

Movement to McLeod's right caught his eye. He spun and found the Comanchero riding away with a blanket-draped figure across the front of his saddle and the mules trailing.

'Carlotta!' The name tore from McLeod's lips before the recognition was clear in his mind. He raised the Colt and started to fire, then hesitated and aimed more carefully and higher to avoid hitting Carlotta. His hand wavered with growing weakness. He took a deep breath, steadied and squeezed the trigger.

The Comanchero jerked forward and grabbed his left arm. He dropped the mules' lead line but righted himself and spurred his horse away. Carlotta's long, raven hair, now matted with blood and dirt, hung down beside the saddle, swinging with the lunging of the horse.

McLeod's strength was ebbing. He carefully aligned the sights just above the collar of the Comanchero and began to squeeze. Thundercloud lunged off the ground and bowled McLeod back before he could fire. He dragged himself on top of McLeod and locked his hands around his throat. Blood poured from a ragged hole in the Comanche's right thigh.

McLeod's attempts to knock the Comanche off him were no more effective than swatting gnats in the air. Even as his vision failed and he slipped toward unconsciousness, he was aware of smells. The strange thought hit him that the tobacco he smelled on the man killing him smelled like the same kind of dark Mexican cigars he smoked. As his hands slid away from Thundercloud and fell to his side, they landed on metal. With his very last reserve of strength, Quentin McLeod eared back the hammer of his Colt, tilted the muzzle upward and squeezed the trigger.

Thundercloud jerked but crushed McLeod's throat more tightly than ever. The Colt slipped from McLeod's hand. Everything went black.

NINE

The bright Texas sun seared McLeod's eyes no matter which way he turned his head. Nor would the smothering weight across his body go away. His mouth was as dry as the deserts he had crossed with the cavalry. From head to toe Quentin McLeod hurt even worse than when the shell fragment had ripped his scalp away during the War. Gradually his view of the world began to clear and sharpen. Being alive was a surprise, not necessarily a pleasant one at the moment.

Someone was on top of him. Black hair lay across part of his face. *Carlotta!* No. The smell was wrong. Smoke . . . tobacco . . . animal fat. Not Carlotta. With his good right hand, McLeod strained against the body. It felt as heavy as a horse to him. At last the body rocked then tumbled off of him.

His left arm wouldn't work. He closed his eyes and gritted his teeth in pain. The world faded away again, a welcome relief. Later the bright sun burned into his eyes and yanked him unpleasantly back awake. Something moved in his mouth. He breathed in and desperately tried to stand. Something went into his windpipe. He sputtered and gagged, tried to clear his throat and to breathe. *Flies!* They scrambled around inside his mouth then flew out. McLeod's gagging turned into coughing that racked his body with more pain. He struggled to remember where he was. What had happened? *The body!*

McLeod turned his head to the body beside him. The Comanche who had been trying to choke McLeod when he passed out lay there, his eyes wide open toward the sun. Flies crawled over each other at a bullet hole just below Thundercloud's left armpit. Memory of the events – it must have been yesterday afternoon – came flooding back.

Carlotta! McLeod jerked to sit up, but fell back in pain. His shoulder! It was agony to move his head far enough to see. His sudden movement startled the flies into the air, their buzz adding an eerie new sound to the bewildering landscape of slaughter. The sight of the bloody mess almost caused him to pass out again.

The Comanchero had taken Carlotta, McLeod remembered. He had to find them. Carefully he tested his left arm. The fingers worked although pain shot all the way to his shoulder when he moved his fingers. He could bend the arm at the elbow, but not very far. The bullet had missed the bone. The dead Comanche lying on him must have pressured the wound enough to stop him from bleeding to death.

McLeod could see his horse standing ground-hitched nearby. Further away the mules picked at the sparse grass. His fuzzy mind struggled with the matter of the mules. They had been behind the Comanchero when McLeod shot. Then he remembered the Comanchero jerking forward at his shot. The Comanchero was hit. Carlotta, if she was alive, might be lying on the Staked Plains.

McLeod struggled to clear his thoughts. Now he had to get up and treat his wounds so he could go after Carlotta. On the second try McLeod succeeded in sitting up. The pain didn't stop, but after a few minutes the world stopped spinning. His shoulder and head throbbed in unison. His head hurt so badly that it was hard for him to keep his eyes open. He felt all of his head. It didn't seem to be hit, so he couldn't figure out why it hurt so badly. He had to get up!

At last he struggled to his feet and staggered the few steps to his horse. He grasped the saddle horn and clung desperately, fighting to keep his knees from buckling. 'Easy, Buck. Easy,' he urged the big horse as it began to edge uneasily away from him.

After a moment McLeod felt steady enough to remove his canteen and drink. Shaking, he caught the rein and leaned on his horse as he walked to where the fire had been. Around the edge of the charred circle, unburned ends of sticks still smoldered. These scraped together would make enough fire to boil water for coffee and to clean his wound.

McLeod passed out once more while the coffee boiled. When he awakened again, the coffee was as black as printers' ink, just what he needed. As the scalding drink eased down his throat, the heat seemed to spread through his entire body. He felt stronger than before, although still shaky and weak.

With the remainder of Carlotta's petticoat retrieved from under the scalped body of the youngest warrior, who had been dressed in Carlotta's dress as part of the trap, McLeod managed to bandage his shoulder well enough to keep the wound covered. Luckily, the rifle ball seemed to have passed cleanly through the flesh.

Coffee began to make McLeod feel more alive, but attempts to chew a piece of jerky proved too painful, so he shaved the jerky into hot water and made an insipid broth that he barely managed to get down. It made him feel stronger, although he realized it might be the thought as much as the actual nourishment that bolstered him.

From his pocket McLeod drew out his last cigar and lit it with a glowing stick from the fire. Even though his body cried out for rest, he must go after Carlotta. McLeod tried to stand but couldn't get off the ground. The move to the fire had sapped the little strength he possessed, and his body had stiffened while he had been sitting. His renewed strength and hope evaporated as he tried to move.

McLeod hobbled awkwardly on his knees and good hand toward Buck. He couldn't put the wounded arm down and tried to get on with just his knees. He tottered and pitched forward on to the wounded shoulder. He screamed in agony. Buck jerked his head and shuffled backward a couple of steps, his ears laid back against his head. McLeod cursed under his breath. The horse was further away than when he began to crawl. He felt like pulling his Colt and putting a slug into the big buckskin's head. Instead he managed to speak soothingly. 'Easy, Buck. Steady, boy.'

The big horse stopped and flopped one ear toward McLeod then extended his nose. McLeod bit his lip and balanced on his knees. He reached his good hand toward Buck. The buckskin sniffed and nuzzled the hand looking for a treat. McLeod eased his hand up the nose and grasped the bridle. 'Easy, fellow,' he cooed. 'Come here.'

He tugged slightly on the bridle and breathed a sigh of relief when Buck stepped close enough that he could grab the stirrup. He steeled himself. He had to get up and mount Buck with one try or he would lie here and die. To die would leave Carlotta in the hands of the Comanchero or else lying out on the Staked Plains for scavengers.

He let the reins slide through his fingers as he grabbed the stirrup and pulled. Although the pain was worse than any other he had ever experienced, he couldn't stop. He started to scream but stopped himself lest he spook the horse. Then he was up on his feet. He hung tightly on to the saddle and laid his throbbing head against the leather, hot from sunlight. Waves of nausea washed over him and almost drove him back to his knees.

For once McLeod wished he rode a horse smaller than Buck's sixteen-and-a-half hands. He managed to raise his hand to Buck's mane but couldn't pull himself up with it. Again he leaned against the big horse and gathered his strength, his eyes closed tightly against the sun. The smells of leather, blood and sweat mingled.

He had to make it on to Buck or die here. A wave of dizziness hit him. He grasped the saddle more tightly. The image of Carlotta across the Comanchero's saddle came to him. He clenched his teeth and willed the dizziness away. He grasped Buck's mane in front of the saddle with his right hand and pulled as he lunged upward. His body swung too far to the left. He teetered then started to fall. Instinctively he grabbed with his left hand. With this hold he managed to flop his leg across the saddle, but the worst pain yet racked him as he hung on to the saddle horn. After a minute he worked his toes into the stirrups and kicked Buck into motion, pointing him toward the path of the tracks left by the Comanchero's horse.

Up on the cap rock, he managed to lift his head and

focus his eyes. The clear tracks of a single horse headed toward the south-west. He turned Buck on to the trail. The tracks wavered for a short distance then straightened, telling McLeod that the Comanchero had been conscious and in control of his horse at this point.

Looking ahead, the Staked Plains stretched to the horizon. The wind-blown undulation of the brownish-tan grass was the only movement. The deep blue of the sky was unbroken except for the fiery disc of the sun. McLeod spurred Buck into a fast walk and again laid his head back on the dark-brown mane and groaned, wavering between consciousness and unconsciousness.

Through the haze inside his head, McLeod became aware that Buck had stopped. It took a couple of minutes for him to fight himself alert enough to notice that they were stopped by the ashes of a fire. Thin wisps of smoke rose from a few charred chunks of buffalo chips. Strips of bloody cloth lay in the edge of the ashes. In bloodstained grass at the end of a depression where a body had lain, several long, black hairs stuck, plastered to the grass. McLeod raged in anger, but there was nothing he could do.

He looked around more carefully. Numerous tracks left the grass pressed to the ground. One horse but over several hours, McLeod could tell. The Comanchero must have spent the night here and couldn't be that far ahead. The Comanchero had taken time to clear a circle, cutting grass down to the roots in order to build a fire that wouldn't set the prairie on fire and signal his presence to anyone else on the Staked Plains. The Comanchero's wound couldn't be too serious, this told McLeod. But

McLeod took solace in the absence of a body, which meant that Carlotta must still be alive.

He ached fiercely from head to toe. His breath almost scorched his lips, even through his thickening mustache. Fever must be gaining a strong hold on his body. Shapes and lines were distorted, and his mind functioned terribly slowly. His mouth and throat were as parched as the dry plain. If only he could lie down for a few minutes! But he knew he would never be able to get back up into the saddle if he did. The Comanchero had Carlotta, and she was alive. He must go on.

TEN

The sound of horses blowing cut through McLeod's sleep. He struggled to pull himself out of the haze, gradually making out the figures of two dozen, blue-clad buffalo soldiers deployed in line to meet him. Black faces stared at him in stony silence. Spencer carbines lay across the troopers' left arms, apparently in casual rest, but McLeod noticed that every soldier rested his thumb on the hammer and his finger on the trigger.

McLeod's gaze finally settled on a pair of bare feet protruding from a screen made by two soldiers holding up a blanket. He blinked as the scene wavered into and out of focus. A small man in a leather jacket and blue army uniform pants crouched to work over the person lying behind the blanket, and then McLeod noticed a tall slender officer who looked neat enough to be on a parade ground rather than out on the Staked Plains. The officer was standing beside the screen and glaring at him. His gunmetal-gray eyes looked as fierce and dangerous as the big bores of the troopers' carbines.

When McLeod recognized the big but feminine feet which extended from behind the blanket, he struggled to swallow then spurred Buck toward the blanket.

In one motion, two dozen troopers shifted their Spencer carbines to their shoulders and leveled their muzzles toward McLeod. The noise of twenty-four hammers cocking made him pull Buck up, but his eyes remained glued to the figure on the ground. 'Carlotta!' His sunken eyes turned to the major. His voice rasped, barely audible. 'Is she. . . ?'

'She's alive,' the major answered. His hard eyes never wavered.

'That's him!'

The words worked their way through to McLeod's understanding. He grasped his saddle horn to hang on and turned toward the voice. An even taller man emerged into view. White bandages showed where his black shirt was torn away from his left shoulder. McLeod felt he should recognize him, but his mind was struggling too hard to cut through the haze to think too much about it right now.

'He's the one I told you about,' the man told the major.

McLeod struggled to pull his pistol when he recognized the man. 'You!'

'Keep your hands on the saddle, mister,' the officer snapped at McLeod.

McLeod gave up on the Colt and raised his legs to spur Buck toward the Comanchero. A burly black sergeant grabbed Buck's reins right next to the bit; the big horse sidestepped and slung his head angrily. The muscles below the sergeant's rolled-up cuff stood out rigidly like big ropes. He spoke soothingly to the horse, but his eyes were as hard and dark as obsidian when he turned them on McLeod. Buck jerked and danced trying to break away from the soldier. McLeod leaned forward and held on to Buck's neck and the saddle horn with all his might but still almost fell off. The jarring sent whole new waves of pain through McLeod. Carbine muzzles followed McLeod as troopers prepared to blast him from his saddle.

'Stand easy!' The officer barked.

McLeod managed to sit up on Buck and yelled at the officer, 'He's a Comanchero! He was with the Comanches that did this to Carlotta.'

The major's face flushed red. 'We know Ian Richards. None of us knows you.'

A small man with fiery red sideburns and captain's bars on his shoulders strode forward, an angry sneer on his face. 'I know him. Quentin McLeod,' the captain said. 'Rebel turned US Cavalry during the War. One of the worst of a sorry lot I had the misfortune to command. I'm not surprised to see what he's turned out to be.' The captain's lips twisted, as if even mentioning McLeod and the Galvanized Yankees was distasteful.

McLeod shook his head to clear the fog that kept trying to creep back into his head. 'Lieutenant Madsen?' he asked.

'Captain Madsen!' the small officer snapped angrily. He turned to the Major. 'I would arrest him.'

'Arrest me?' McLeod asked incredulously. He pointed toward Ian Richards. 'I took Carlotta from that man and Comanches!'

Ian Richards stepped forward. 'I rescued the woman from this man and some savages. I was wounded in the process.'

His eyes locked with McLeod's for a brief moment, then shifted back to the tall major. 'Check his pack mules. See what he's carrying,' he suggested. McLeod saw a hint of a smile at the corners of the Comanchero's lips.

The major nodded to a small, wrinkled, civilian muleskinner on the edge of the group.

'Carlotta and I took the mules from this man,' McLeod protested.

'Check this man's mules,' the major repeated, his voice impatient.

McLeod slumped in his saddle, feeling every ounce of the pain and fatigue from the last four days. The muleskinner and a young private in a new, too large uniform loosened the diamond hitches holding the packs. One crate slipped through the two men's hands and burst open on the ground. The Texas sun reflected brightly off the brass housings of six new Henry rifles as they spilled on to the prairie.

Hardened soldiers gasped. These repeating rifles in the hands of Comanches would mean that the soldiers would be badly out-gunned in combat. Angry red suffused the major's face. 'I think that answers our questions. You are under arrest.'

The man who had been kneeling by the blanket approached the major. He was small, not over five feet, four inches, and exceptionally slight of frame, his brown face deeply tanned and wrinkled. Brown eyes, seemingly too large for his small face, shone hard with fury. 'Major Byrd.'

The major turned to him. 'Doctor?'

'She's badly beaten. She has a chance to make it. Not a good chance – but a chance.'

The major's face seemed to harden even more as he turned to the big sergeant. 'Prepare a litter for her.' The two nearest troopers lowered their carbines and turned to rig a rectangle of canvas into a litter to pull behind one of the cavalry mounts. The doctor remained by the major's side, hesitated before he spoke again. 'Major.'

'Yes?'

'She has been . . . violated . . . brutally,' he added, speaking through tight lips.

An angry mutter spread through the group of men.

McLeod struggled to make out the doctor's words. 'Vio. . . ?' The meaning of the doctor's words finally came clear. 'You son of a bitch!' McLeod snarled and leaped Buck toward Richards.

A lanky corporal stepped forward and clubbed McLeod with the butt of his carbine. Sharp pain exploded inside McLeod's head. The sky rolled overhead and Buck's head was suddenly above his own. There was a brief kaleidoscope of colors before the world faded away once more.

Ian Richards pointed toward blue cloth that protruded from McLeod's saddle-bag and asked, 'What's that, Major?'

Major Byrd followed Richards's point to the blue and nodded. 'Corporal Baker.'

The tall corporal who had hit McLeod stepped to the bag and pulled out Carlotta's blue dress, holding it up for all to see, now tattered, torn and bloody. Voices rose in angry tones.

Richards stepped forward and asked, his voice a growl, 'We don't have to waste time arresting this man, do we? Why bother?'

The troopers' eyes turned to their commander.

'Easy Ian,' the major answered. 'Even he gets a trial.'

Off to the side of the group, the muleskinner watched closely, and then turned to the young private who helped him with mules. 'I don't know, sonny. I just don't know.'

'What do you mean, Mr Ethan?' the young private asked.

'I may forget a person, but nary a mule,' the old man said and rubbed his chin. 'I seed them mules around before. Seems peculiar.'

'Where, Mr Ethan?'

Ethan Thompson stood deep in memory.

Ethan didn't like or trust any Englishman. But it was the way Ian Richards treated horses and mules that Ethan really disliked. The damned Englishman with his fancy tea-sipping manners and fine clothes might impress most of the people in New Mexico, but Ethan Thompson had treated sores from pack saddles on Richards's mules and whip cuts on horses. As far as he was concerned, any man who mistreated his stock was a low-down sorry scoundrel.

The young soldier stared expectantly at the old skinner. Ethan Thompson spat tobacco at a horsefly on the tall grass near him and wiped his mouth. 'That's officer and law business. Don't hold with mixing in it.'

ELEVEN

The burning pain of a hot cloth bathing the bullet wound on McLeod's shoulder woke him. *Carlotta*! But it wasn't Carlotta. A thin stream of sunlight from a small window high on a thick gray stone wall fell on to McLeod's face. He squinted and jerked his head, the quick movement causing him to groan in pain. I must have dreamed it all, he thought. But the iron bars of a jail cell told him it wasn't a dream.

The army surgeon whom McLeod had seen on the plains used strips of white cloth to bind a soft pad tightly over his shoulder wound. 'Good thing you stayed out a while. This would have hurt like forty kinds of hell if you had been awake.' The last pull on the cloth securing his bandage caused McLeod to wince. The small doctor pointed to clothing stacked neatly on the end of the cot. 'Put those on.'

'New clothes?' McLeod asked, surprised.

'I cut what was left of your shirt loose, which wasn't much loss, and Captain Madsen insists you have other pants. Wants you in no part of a US Army uniform.' The surgeon rolled his eyes and snickered as if he thought the captain ridiculous. He closed his medical bag and set it on the floor, sat in the straight-backed wooden chair beside McLeod's cot and leaned back with his fingers locked around his knees. 'You're some messed up, boy. Tell me how these wounds happened.'

McLeod wasn't sure why he wasted time with the surgeon since everyone seemed to believe Ian Richards, but it felt good to talk. He spoke while getting gingerly into the gray woolen pants and red cotton shirt. The surgeon sat back and listened, only occasionally interrupting with questions.

When McLeod finished, the surgeon barraged him with questions. 'What is the lady's name? . . . was Mrs Mainord conscious when you last saw her? . . . exactly what had happened in the fight? . . . why did you have her dress?'

McLeod carefully repositioned his body where he sat on the cot and leaned back against the wall. The surgeon listened to McLeod's answers without comment then asked, 'Where is Mrs Mainord from?'

The clatter of an army patrol passing by attracted McLeod's attention for a moment and evoked images of earlier days. When he thought about the doctor's questions, he was surprised at how little he had learned in some ways during his and Carlotta's few days together. Yet in a way he had learned so very much. Certainly he knew all he needed to know to fall very much in love with Carlotta Mainord.

He answered Doctor Carpenter, who had waited patiently, 'Texas. Fredericksburg. Or at least she told me about when she had gone to school in Fredericksburg. Her husband, Grady, died as a prisoner of war. I don't know much more. We were too busy running to talk much.

Besides, we didn't hit it off too well at first. She didn't like the color of my pants,' McLeod said, smiling wryly at the memory.

The surgeon sat listening and spoke little. Without his hat, he turned out to have even less hair than McLeod. When he started to leave, McLeod caught him by the arm. His eyes burned into the surgeon's. 'Now tell me about Carlotta. Where and how is she?'

The surgeon sat back down in the straight chair. 'She's at Ian Richards's ranch.'

McLeod bolted to his feet and nearly fainted from the pain that movement caused. Doctor Carpenter caught McLeod by the arm and steadied him.

'Ian Richards's ranch?' McLeod asked incredulously. 'Good Lord, man—'

The surgeon used McLeod's arm to guide him back to the cot. 'It wasn't my idea,' the doctor explained in a mollifying tone, 'but there aren't that many comfortable places in Fort Sumner. I check on her a couple of times each day and besides' – the surgeon chuckled softly – 'the Señora Baeza is duenna.'

'Duenna?' McLeod asked.

The doctor explained, 'Chaperone or governess. In Spanish families they carefully supervise proper young ladies. Believe me, I'd rather have Señora Baeza than a squadron of cavalry protecting any lady of mine. Mrs Mainord is safe.'

The doctor's smile faded. His face clouded. 'I wish I felt as confident about her recovery. She's awfully beaten up and still unconscious.'

Señora Baeza sat impassively by the heavy bed in the

darkened room with Carlotta Mainord. The *señora* dressed as somberly as usual: black dress, black shawl and the appropriately somber demeanor which was largely responsible for her having become trusted duenna instead of mother of her own daughters. She hesitated to leave, but it was time for her daily devotions. No one else, she felt quite sure, was on the ranch. She decided that she could safely go to the chapel that the Englishman Richards had reluctantly set up for her in his rambling ranch house.

A very light pair of eyes in a very pale face watched as the black-clad duenna swept down the hall toward the chapel. Her walk was surprisingly springy for an elderly señora. The tall figure of the ranch's owner emerged into the hall. Ian Richards, now clean and crisp in the black suit, starched white shirt, and black tie of a prosperous businessman and rancher, moved as smoothly and silently as a cat. His fingers closed and opened nervously, much like a cat would sheath and bare its claws. He entered the room where Carlotta lay and walked to her side. The dim light of two candles across the room cast shadows that made his gaunt face seem even more sinister. Shadow linked the already merging eyebrows. 'So, your name is Carlotta Mainord. Well, Mrs Mainord, as that quack calls you, you will be mine. I want you to get well. I want more of you before I get to hear you scream and beg while they take you off in the slave wagon to a Mexican whore house.' As he talked, he slid one of the long hands under the thick woolen blanket and circled Carlotta's nipple. A slight sound of rustling cloth in the hall alerted him that the duenna he had already come to detest was returning.

By the time Señora Baeza bustled into the room, Ian Richards was sitting in the chair by the big Bible, hat in hand, his head bowed as if in prayer. He stood respectfully and bowed his head slightly. '*Buenos dias*, Señora Baeza,' he greeted in very proper tone. 'Our guest rests well.'

The duenna pulled her shawl over the lower portion of her face, gave the ranch owner a slight curtsy and nodded. Richards couldn't help feeling awkward. The old woman made him nervous. He bowed slightly. 'Good evening, señora. I will be in town. Please send someone if there should be any change in our guest's condition.'

The señora didn't respond. When Ian Richards was gone, she quickly crossed herself, went to the bedside and straightened the blanket back to the way she had left it.

Carlotta stirred slightly but her eyes remained closed. Señora Baeza looked around the room, walked to the door, looked warily up and down the hall and returned to Carlotta's side. 'He's gone, Señora Mainord,' she said as she gently stroked Carlotta's hair.

The stable, even with its stacks of hay, bags of grain and assortment of tack, was one of the neatest places in Fort Sumner. Ethan Thompson took better care of his mules than most people took of their families. As far as that went, he lavished more care on his mules than he had his family when he had one.

The small, wrinkled old man sat on a wooden chair leaning against one of the supporting cedar poles, nubbed remains of limbs still present. He smoked his short clay pipe while he worked saddle-soap into a mule collar. His faded jeans and butternut shirt were clean but rumpled. Red suspenders seemed to hold the whole outfit together. His worn boots hadn't seen any attempt at shining in years and looked like it.

79

An even smaller man stepped into the yellow light of the single lantern. Ethan barely looked up. 'Evening, Doc.'

Doctor Carpenter moved another wooden chair from the wall to a spot directly in front of Ethan. He sat and leaned back, eyes closely watching the stable owner. 'Ethan, Private Martin said I should talk to you about some mules.'

The old man stopped his brushing and looked directly at the doctor. Ethan heard a mule in the back of the stable paw the gate of a stall but noted that the animal didn't sound serious. He returned his attention to Doctor Carpenter. The two of them had been together on a number of campaigns across the West. Ethan Thompson knew perfectly well that Dr Joseph Carpenter didn't need anyone's advice on either picking or caring for mules. 'Mules, Doc?'

The doctor shifted his straight chair and took his pocketknife out to whittle, as if expecting a long conversation. 'Those that Quentin McLeod had with him when we found him on the Staked Plains.'

The sound of heavy footsteps, heel-first, army-style, approached McLeod's cell. McLeod barely opened his eye to see who was coming. He was sorer than he had ever been in his life. The shoulder felt better from the attention of the surgeon the previous day, but the accumulation of the beatings and wounds over the last few days had taken its toll. Unless coffee or food was the reason for the army jailer's visit, Quentin McLeod would just as soon ignore it.

'Visitor,' the gruff, black corporal announced, then

turned on his heel and left the two alone.

McLeod reached gingerly up, pushed his hat off his face and peered uncertainly at the other person. He was better able to focus his eyes today.

A small, very dark man dressed in black from boots to wide-brimmed hat stood by the jailer. His image prodded McLeod's memory but failed to register clearly. The man stood patiently with a crooked grin that seemed friendly despite the jagged scar from the corner of his mouth to the edge of his left eye.

'Why, you Florida river rat!' the visitor exclaimed in a jesting tone. 'Damn you if you can't remember me after all the times I saved you from those Yankees.'

McLeod sat up as fast as he could manage and peered more closely. He scrambled to get to his feet, pushing with his right arm. A smile split his battered face. 'Well I'll be—! Tobias Wilcox! Just when you think things can't get worse, you show up. You nearly caused those damned blue bellies to kill me a hundred times or so. You must be here now to finish the job.'

McLeod hobbled to the bars as fast as he could and reached out to grab the hand of the little man. The man grabbed McLeod and pulled him up to the bars for as much of a hug as could be given through the bars. McLeod returned the embrace, although the squeeze and the little man pounding on his back hurt badly. He felt tears well up in his eyes at the sight of his old friend. 'What in blue blazes are you doing here?' he asked through a wide smile. 'Don't tell me Tobias Wilcox finally decided to become a Galvanized Yankee?'

The little man laughed. 'No way. I'm here with a cattle herd. Charles Goodnight, Oliver Loving and a few of us fools delivered a herd to feed all these Navajos they got penned up here.'

'From Texas?' McLeod asked.

'Where else?' the visitor responded in a voice deeper than one would expect from such a small man. 'I told you I'd never leave Texas again if I ever got out of that prison.'

McLeod limped to the corner of his cot and sat down. For a moment he had to sit very still to fight off dizziness. When he finally spoke, his voice was sober. 'I didn't expect to find a friendly face here.'

Wilcox pulled a chair up to the edge of the cell and sat as close to McLeod as possible. 'I must be the only friendly face around right now. You're about the most unpopular fellow I ever saw. Tell me about all this.'

McLeod leaned back against the wall. 'I came down just to look over the chances of hide-hunting on the Llano and. . . .'

Fifteen minutes later, Wilcox stood up. 'Can't stay long. They almost wouldn't let me in here in the first place.'

McLeod hobbled back to the bars and seized his friend's hand. 'It's good to see you, Tobias. I didn't think you would make it out of that prison during the war.' He paused a moment before continuing in quiet earnest. 'You would never have lived had you not joined the Galvanized Yankees and gotten medical care. We were all glad you did it.'

Tobias Wilcox looked Quentin McLeod directly in the eye, his expression and his voice without the bravado McLeod remembered to be so common with the little Texan. 'McLeod, I'll try to help you, but I don't know what I can do. That Ian Richards fellow is buying liquor for folks like it was water. He's talking about what an outrage it is to waste a trial on you. I think that red-headed Captain Madsen is part of it, too.'

McLeod held on to the bars with both hands to steady himself. 'Madsen was my commanding officer when I joined the Yankees on the plains. He hated all of us. In fact he seemed to hate everybody and everything.'

McLeod let his memory drift back to unpleasant times. 'You know the type.' Anger flashed in his eyes at the memories. 'Like those prison guards that never heard a minie ball but tried to show how tough they were by pushing prisoners around. Not like the Yanks in the lines. You fought them but they were all right.' Then McLeod snapped back to the present situation. 'Madsen isn't right in the head.'

Wilcox nodded. 'He's got it in for you. Doesn't like us Texans too much, either. You take care, River Rat.'

McLeod didn't feel quite as lonely as before, but he had an empty feeling about the Comanchero and Madsen. At least Wilcox had promised to get Goodnight or Loving to check on Carlotta.

The one lantern down the hall from McLeod cast little light into his cell. Some draft of air caused the flame to waver. The cell was dim, even for McLeod, whose eyes had adjusted to the area. He sensed a presence although he didn't hear anyone. He lay still and watched carefully. At first glance the face outside his cell was shrouded in shadows, but finally the shape of bushy sideburns came into focus.

The soldier in uniform grasped the bars of the cell. His hands were visible, but the face remained in shadow. 'Rebel, you're not going to last the night. I wanted to see

83

your face when you knew it.' He paused for a long moment and then continued, sarcasm heavy in his voice, 'I'm afraid the officer of the day just might become indisposed later when you're on your way out to a noose.'

'Why, Madsen?' McLeod asked, still without moving.

The army officer's fingers squeezed tightly around the bars; his face pushed forward. McLeod wished he could move as he normally did. He would spring forward and crush Madsen's neck with his bare hands.

'Why?' Madsen's voice dripped with hatred. 'I hate every one of you scroungers. Galvanized Yankees! You ruined my career. My father paid good money for my spot at West Point. We get a war just when I need it, and then I wind up out on the godless prairies with you rebels.'

McLeod sat up stiffly. 'They sent you out there because you were no good, Madsen.'

'Captain Madsen! Captain! You rebel heathen!' The captain stamped the bottom of the cell door with his heel. His angry face leaned forward into the light, almost as red as his sideburns it seemed.

Now McLeod knew he had told Tobias right. Madsen was crazy.

The captain raged, pacing back and forth in front of McLeod's cell and angrily pounded his fist into his other hand. 'First I get stuck with you rebels and now with these baboons. Colored troops. Baby-sitting godless red savages. All because I missed the war with you rebel trash!' Madsen started stomping away then turned back and thrust his finger toward McLeod. 'But I get even with you tonight.'

TWELVE

The Oasis was an overly pretentious name for the squat, dirt-floored, adobe hovel with four tables, three with mismatched chairs and a fourth with no chairs except discarded packing crates. Two makeshift bars had been created by stacking still more of the abandoned crates in rows.

Drinkers had a choice of lukewarm beer or an ugly mixture of grain alcohol, water and cheap tobacco, unless they could afford a half-dollar a shot for a better grade reputed to be Tennessee whiskey. Fifty cents was a day's wages for many of the patrons of the Oasis.

A tall Texan with trail-worn but clean clothes and a leather vest made from the hair of a mottled longhorn sat in a four-handed poker game at one of the tables with chairs. He shared his bottle with Doctor Carpenter, the only army person present. The doctor was still nursing the first shot of Tennessee whiskey thirty minutes into a poker game with the tall Texan, a dapper salesman trying to sell to the army and a local rancher of obvious Mexican lineage.

The players squinted to read the cards in the yellow light of two coal oil lanterns. Tobacco smoke hung heavily in the room, lending an unreal cast to the scene. A cacophony of smells – sweaty bodies, cheap whiskey, stale tobacco smoke, chewing tobacco spat as often on to the floor as into the old rusty buckets which pretended as cuspidors, the odor of the lanterns, cheap perfume, horse sweat – bombarded the senses.

Ian Richards kept up a harangue as he liberally spread the more expensive whiskey among the bar's patrons. 'I agree with you fellows that hanging is much too good for this Comanchero. We really should save tax dollars by doing him in ourselves.'

Jared Sparkman, a visiting attorney from Las Vegas, New Mexico, his brown, woolen suit wrinkled from travel, cleared his throat and spoke with the assured air of one accustomed to having an attentive audience. 'I agree with everything you express, Mr Richards, except I must object to mob violence. The law will handle this brigand.'

The crowd became quiet. Ian Richards stopped his movement and stared at the attorney. His long fingers stroked the bottle from which he had been pouring as he spoke quietly but in a voice that clearly bespoke threat, allowing his eyes to take in the audience and draw them in as his backers. 'Mr Sparkman, do you want to be known as the only defender of this savage?'

Sparkman loosened his collar and fidgeted. 'No, I'm not defending him,' Sparkman was quick to aver.

One farmer better dressed than most asked, 'You don't reckon a jury would turn him loose, do you, Mr Richards?'

Richards topped off the farmer's drink and raised his voice loud enough that no one could miss his words. 'You never know, Mr Hawkins, do you? Get a bunch of pettifogging lawyers and an addlepated judge, who knows what nonsense might come out of it?'

A heavy-set teamster in a red, woolen shirt with wide, leather suspenders held his glass out to Ian Richards as he spoke. 'Caught him red-handed with two mule loads of rifles, didn't they? Who else but red devils would he sell to out on the Staked Plains?'

Ian Richards poured more glasses of whiskey, raised the nearly empty bottle to signal the bartender for a replacement and continued in his precise English accent. 'You men cannot understand the way I feel without seeing what I saw. I had slipped up close to the Comanche camp. Quentin McLeod raped her right in front of those howling savages and was about to let them have their way with her when I opened fire. I shot the Comanchero and got enough bullets into the rest of the red devils to scare them away long enough for me to grab the woman and run.'

Richards paused and sipped on his whiskey. The sound of the cards being shuffled at the table was clearly audible. A lone horseman clopped by, seeming loud in the drawn-out silence. Richards allowed the silence to linger dramatically before continuing, 'I just wish I had killed the bloody lout instead of wounding him. I was using a strange rifle,' he explained, 'an old Hawken I had picked up from Comanches with whom I had an earlier brush.'

Richards turned his attention to the tall Texan sitting across the table from Doctor Carpenter. 'I guess you Texans would know what to do with a Comanchero, wouldn't you?' he asked as he rose and moved over beside the table where the card game was taking place.

The Texan ignored Richards for a long moment. Then he lifted his glass as in a toast, sipped the whiskey appreciatively and spoke in a deep drawl. 'If I was in Texas, I'd deal with him, but this is New Mexico. None of my business, I guess.'

Richards glared at the Texan. The Texan studied his cards, studiously ignoring the Englishman's hostile demeanor.

'You're sure about what you saw?' Doctor Carpenter asked.

Richards seized the opportunity to turn attention away from the Texan. 'I saw it as clearly as I see you people in here. It was I who put that bullet into the Comanchero's shoulder and also several Comanches. I ran the red devils off long enough to rescue the woman and get out.'

'You worked from behind cover?' the Texan asked.

The audience hung on each word. Richards eagerly picked up on the opening. 'I did. You should have seen the devils scatter when I dropped the Comanchero and then hit several of them. They didn't know who I was or from where I was shooting.'

'From where were you shooting?' the Texan asked mildly.

'From cover,' Richards repeated. 'They never knew what hit them.'

When Richards paused, the Texan spoke to Doctor Carpenter just loudly enough to be overheard by anyone who cared. 'I never been up on the Staked Plains, myself. I'd always thought it was flat and grassy, that you could see for miles. A fellow learns new things every day.'

Richards pivoted away from the table and moved through the crowd filling glasses, easing himself and his audience further away from the Texan and Doctor Carpenter. 'The only way we can ever get this place civilized,' he proclaimed loudly, 'is to get rid of vermin like this McLeod. You fellows have to leave your women alone sometimes while you go make a living, don't you? How safe can it be for them with a man like him alive?'

He moved ever further away from the poker table, filling empty glasses. 'I had never seen the woman before, but I'm sure she's a real Texas lady. McLeod treated her like common trash.'

The two other players left the poker table, leaving Doctor Carpenter and the Texan to themselves. 'What do you think, Mr Loving?' the doctor asked quietly.

'Call me Oliver,' the Texan encouraged. 'I think this Richards must be some plainsman and some shootist. He says he slipped up on a Comanchero and a whole Comanche party in the middle of an open plain, shot this McLeod fellow as well as several Comanches, and did it with a single shot, muzzle-loading Hawken he had picked up from the Comanches. He must be hell on wheels.'

Across the room, Ian Richards and followers surged angrily out the door.

Doctor Carpenter went to the window to watch the crowd forming in the street. 'What are you going to do, Mr Loving?' he asked.

'Finish my drink,' the Texan responded and dealt a solitaire hand. Doctor Carpenter picked up his hat and hurried out a side door. Oliver Loving could hear the Englishman outside haranguing, 'Those red devils were born red devils, but Quentin McLeod is what he chose to become!'

A gaudily clad, heavily made-up woman emerged from a dark corner where she had avoided the crowd. She came to the table, picked up the doctor's unfinished drink and looked inquisitively at Oliver Loving.

'Help yourself, ma'am,' he told the woman. He poured her glass full again when she drained the glass. 'Care for a game of cards?' he drawled. The odor of a sweaty female, very distinctive from that of any man, made its way to his nostrils. He liked the smell of female sweat. It seemed a nice honest odor to him and excited him physically more than the sight of a woman.

She ignored the question and looked nervously around the room. 'That Englishman scares the hell out of me!'

The Texan raised his eyebrows but said nothing as he turned the ace of diamonds face up, then laid out six other cards in a precisely spaced row.

THIRTEEN

The army bacon and beans from Quentin McLeod's supper weren't sitting comfortably on his stomach. His nose told him he wouldn't be the first occupant of the poorly ventilated jail to lose his supper, if he did so. He lay stiff, sore and tired, but he was fully awake. The growing crowd milled around a large fire in Fort Sumner's one street, a half block from the front of the jail. No one remembered the fire being built. It was just there. Bottles of the better whiskey from the Oasis circulated freely through the crowd.

The flickering of the fire and squares of yellow light from the lanterns inside the Oasis dimly lit the scene. In the uncharacteristically humid air, the haze of smoke and dust combined with the warm inner glow of whiskey to create a sense of unreality. The whiskey, the fire and the excitement combined to warm the men despite the cool air.

Ian Richards drifted through the crowd like an unnaturally elongated shadow, quietly agitating one huddle of men, then another. The level of noise grew steadily until it sounded like the first rumblings of

91

floodwater rushing down a desert arroyo.

From time to time Quentin McLeod could hear the voice he recognized as that of the Comanchero. He worked frantically to loosen the leg of his cot, despite the agony the effort caused to his bullet-torn shoulder and battered body. The cot's legs were set into the stones of the floor, the head and foot pieces extending through the wall to form the head and foot of the cots in the next cell. McLeod worked on first one piece and then another, desperate to find some kind of a weapon.

His heart almost stood still for a moment when he felt the cot frame come loose. He pushed and pulled harder and harder, panting from exertion and nervousness. Outside, the crowd grew more boisterous.

McLeod had heard nothing from Captain Madsen since his earlier visit to the cell and figured that Madsen had guard duty alone. Finally another piece of the cot frame came completely free, but not before blood was seeping from the wound on McLeod's shoulder. He worked the pegs that joined the frame free but left them loosely in place. This done, he sat on the floor with his back against the wall and fell immediately asleep.

McLeod jerked awake as voices roared toward the jail. He quickly took the bed apart and laid the two-by-six and legs beside him. The door slammed hard against the wall of the cell area. For a moment lamps illuminated the area more brightly, but bodies soon came between the lights and McLeod's cell, leaving the area dim again. The crowd surged toward McLeod's cell. Hot air and body stench rushed over him like a tidal wave.

McLeod cringed against the wall as if paralyzed by fear as the men pushed and shoved each other, eager to be the first into the cell. He moved the bed leg close to his side and grasped the rough end of the longer piece, brushing his fingers over the saw strokes. He flexed the muscles of his shoulder twice and shook them loose trying to ignore the pain, took a deep breath and exhaled smoothly. The time for planning was past.

McLeod rolled his hips and drove the wood forward with all his strength. The men never saw the timber until it caught a big, roughly dressed man in the mouth. Teeth and bones cracked audibly. The wounded man dropped; blood spilled. His howl of pain mingled with the other noises. The men pressed closest against the bars tried to scatter, but others further back pressed too tightly forward to allow anyone out.

McLeod's second target, a chubby man in a business suit, fell writhing on the floor and lost control of his bowels. His fellow lynchers trampled the wounded man, causing him almost as much damage as McLeod's timber. Noise rose to bedlam level. McLeod fought furiously even as he realized he had no real chance. He brought the two-by-six up for another thrust, thought of Carlotta and hoped Tobias Wilcox could watch over her.

His next thrust caught a man in bib overalls in the belly, but others caught and wrested away the beam. Furious men ripped the door open and poured into the cell. McLeod grabbed a bed leg and raised it above his head to wield as a club. The front man covered his head and ducked. McLeod swung with all the strength he had left at the man's leg. The man's knee buckled backward, his scream almost lost in all the yelling from the liquored-up men. Others pressed forward. McLeod managed one more thrust, but his attackers grabbed the post. McLeod yanked desperately, trying to get his weapon clear. It was torn from his hands. He fell to his knees and scrambled for another weapon but then collapsed under the swarm of the mob.

New wounds poured blood down his face and into his mouth. Boots stomped him until he was sure he would die right there in the cell. He struggled to stay conscious; it wasn't in him to give in to his fate.

'Men! Men!' an authoritative voice proclaimed. Through the fog gathering in his brain, McLeod recognized the English accent. 'Save him for a rope. Others can learn from his lesson. Bring him!'

Rough hands jerked McLeod to his feet and propelled him through the door. Blood from the reopened wound on his forehead partially blinded him. He almost passed out from the pain of his old wounds plus those from the beating and stomping in the cell. His head slammed into the door frame as he was pushed and pulled through the door into the jail office. Captain Madsen sat with one hand cuffed to a doorknob and his feet propped comfortably on the desk. He lifted the cup in his free hand in a sarcastic toast to McLeod. 'As you see, Rebel, I can do nothing.'

'To the livery gate!' Richards directed. The crowd surged toward Ethan Thompson's corral where a heavy crosspiece spanned the two fifteen foot high gateposts, providing an excellent impromptu gallows.

'Here, boys!' The English voice directed again. McLeod struggled to lift his head. Someone in the crowd placed rough boards across barrels to create a shaky platform underneath the gallows. Richards leaped easily to the platform and waved a rope with a noose as one might a trophy. The crowd cheered enthusiastically.

McLeod tried to focus his blurry eyes on the Comanchero's face. In the unsteady light from the torches, the shadows on the gaunt face changed rapidly, moving from one eerie shape to another. McLeod shuddered at the evil of the face. The image of Carlotta helpless before this man moved him to search for some way of escape. He could come up with no plan, no ploy to escape hanging.

'Get him up here, boys!' Richards shouted as he tossed the rope over the crosspiece.

Two new sets of hands yanked McLeod's feet from under him and a knee slammed on to his chest as he hit the ground. He fought desperately to breathe. Hands that McLeod couldn't see quickly bound his wrists and feet, jerked him back to a standing position and dumped him on to the platform. Richards snatched the hair along the side of McLeod's head and held him while he looped the rope around his neck. With surprising strength for one so slender, the Englishman yanked McLeod to his feet. He held up a hand for silence.

Bright light from a bonfire partially blinded McLeod and made the scene seem more unreal. He gasped for air but instead inhaled draughts of raw smoke that seared his nose and throat and lungs.

'This is what happens to Comancheros here in Fort Sumner,' Richards shouted as he lifted the rope against McLeod's neck. The crowd roared its approval. Several brandished bottles and shared drinks. Richards began again. 'This man—'

A gunshot split the air. Richards ducked. McLeod struggled to stay upright.

A heavy-set man on a black horse pushed through the stunned crowd. Spectators pushed and shoved to get away from the big horse and its rider. 'Stand easy there, fellows,' the mounted man ordered. 'This old Greener scatters a lot of shot.' He waved a short, double-barreled express gun to emphasize his point. The man's accent and dress identified him as one of the Texans in town. A look into his eyes sobered some in the crowd almost as much as the shotgun. 'Mr Loving over there,' he continued, 'dearly loves any excuse to shoot that old Colt of his.' Eyes followed his point to the lanky figure sitting casually on a brown horse. Oliver Loving smiled and waved a huge old Walker Colt. Other mounted men with drawn guns surrounded the crowd.

'Everyone carrying iron put it on the ground, real careful-like,' the first Texan directed.

Most in the crowd recognized Charles Goodnight, Oliver Loving and their crew of Texas trail drivers. Goodnight waited silently until the weapons were in the street before he announced, 'No one is going to lynch a Texan while I'm in town.'

'This man raped a Texas woman,' Richards argued. 'He was—'

'We don't know that,' Goodnight declared and tilted the muzzle of the shotgun toward Richards's face. 'If a jury finds him guilty, I'll put the rope around his neck and kick the board out from under him myself, but no mob's going to lynch a Texan tonight.'

He waggled the shotgun at Ian Richards. 'Now real careful, you take that rope loose and get this man down. Any accident and there won't be much of you left.'

Richards opened and closed his hands angrily. 'I'll be

damned if—'

'You'll be dead if you don't,' Oliver Loving said and cocked his huge Colt. 'Now don't aggravate me, fellow. You already interrupted a bottle of good whiskey and my card game. I'd like to shoot a Yankee just on principle because of that. Now—' Loving motioned with the barrel of his old pistol toward the rope.

Richards removed the noose and turned.

'Cut him loose and help him down,' Oliver Loving drawled.

Richards gritted his teeth but cut the ropes and helped McLeod down. McLeod clung shakily on to the side of the platform.

Goodnight nudged his mount forward and pointed his shotgun toward McLeod. 'Back to jail with you.'

Riders formed a wall on either side of McLeod as he walked back to the jail, occasionally bracing himself on Charles Goodnight's stirrup. The crowd melted into the night.

Doctor Carpenter pulled the ties of the bandage tight one more time. 'You'll make it. That's a special decoction I got from the Osage Indians when I was stationed at Fort Gibson before the war. You'll heal up faster than you think if you'll give it a chance.'

'I didn't exactly plan that shindig last night,' McLeod told the old doctor and tried to smile.

Outside the cell Tobias Wilcox sat with a shotgun across his lap. Goodnight had demanded that a Texan be on guard henceforth. When the doctor was gone, Wilcox moved his chair closer to the side of the cell. He whispered conspiratorially, as if there might be listeners.

'If Mr Goodnight asks, you're from Jefferson, Texas.'

Wilcox struck a match against his pant leg to light a cigar for McLeod and then himself. 'I had to tell Mr Goodnight you were from Texas to get him to bust up that lynch mob,' Wilcox explained.

'I wondered where he got that idea,' McLeod told Wilcox and tried again to smile.

He thought of Carlotta and tried to remember whether Jewel had ever so occupied his mind. He knew that his rescue the night before was temporary, and that he didn't stand a ghost of a chance before a Fort Sumner jury. What would happen to Carlotta if he were hanged?

FOURTEEN

Two mornings after the lynching attempt, the Texas cabal of Charles Goodnight, Oliver Loving and Tobias Wilcox gathered outside Quentin McLeod's cell. Little light filtered into the cell during the morning. The jail smelled of stale tobacco and alcohol.

Goodnight was muscular and slightly shorter than McLeod. His facial features indicated that he was still in his twenties, but his demeanor was that of a man accustomed to receiving attention and obedience. He came to the point. 'You go on trial tomorrow. So far we can't find a lawyer who will defend you.'

'I'm going to defend you,' Oliver Loving told McLeod.

Goodnight looked at his partner as if he had lost his mind. 'You're what?'

Loving straightened to his full height, several inches taller than McLeod or Goodnight. Loving appeared to be twice Goodnight's age.

'I'm going to defend the man,' Loving repeated cheerfully.

'I appreciate that, Mr Lov—' McLeod began.

'This isn't some bull session with a jug of whiskey in a

99

mesquite shade, Oliver,' Goodnight snapped, interrupting McLeod. 'This man's life is on the line!'

'If no one else will defend me, then I appreciate what Mr Loving can do for me,' McLeod said.

Goodnight often complained that while his partner was the most competent man he had ever known, his unlimited confidence in his abilities and complete lack of fear sometimes put himself and others in unnecessary danger. He considered his partner's offer to defend McLeod to be an extension of this excessive confidence. Goodnight answered McLeod's words but glared at his partner as he spoke. 'This windbag thinks that he can lawyer just because he spouts a few phrases of Latin.'

'That's more than most lawyers out here know,' Loving said and winked at McLeod. 'A little Latin wouldn't hurt you, Charles.'

Goodnight's face turned red. 'You don't even know what those Latin words mean.'

'You think the jurors will know?' Loving asked.

Goodnight ran his fingers angrily through his hair. 'I swear, Oliver. You beat all.'

Goodnight shook his head and walked toward the door. He stopped and turned to face McLeod. 'If you let this windbag represent you, he's got a fool for a client. Don't you realize what's at stake here?' Frustration grew in Goodnight's voice. 'This innocent-until-proven-guilty stuff is a farce. In these people's minds you've already been tried and convicted. You need more lawyering than a few spurts of Latin and what little law Oliver knows from rangering.' Goodnight hesitated as if trying to find more words to bring his partner and McLeod to their senses, then shoved his hat down over his head and stomped away from the cell.

'Charles is a first-rate cattleman, but he does take the world serious,' Loving told McLeod, then sobered. 'Son, he's telling you the truth. I'm no lawyer. I was a Texas Ranger years back, but we didn't pay much attention to formalities in those days. But I figure I'd do better than no one, which is what you have right now. If you know someone else to defend you, you better get him. Time's short.'

McLeod hobbled to the cot and sat down. 'There's no one, Mr Loving.'

Loving slapped his knee, hooked his thumbs under his cowhide vest, and shuffled several quick dance steps. 'Well, hot damn! Let's do it.'

McLeod felt he had to tell Loving. 'There's one thing I think you should know, Mr Loving.' He hesitated. Tobias Wilcox looked hard at McLeod as if trying to discourage him. 'I'm not from Texas. Tobias told Mr Goodnight that to get him to help me.'

Wilcox stared down at the stone floor as if giving it serious study. Loving glared fiercely back and forth at both for a long moment, then laughed and slapped his knee. 'By dog, that's quick thinking, Tobias. But let's don't tell Charles that just yet.'

'Have you had your morning coffee?' Loving asked.

'The guard said they're not furnishing coffee for prisoners or Texans,' Wilcox responded angrily.

Loving straightened to his full height; red suffused his deeply tanned face. 'You tell that blue-bellied coffee cooler that lawyer Loving wants a pot of coffee and three cups. Otherwise he's going to lay a Dragoon Colt barrel along the side of some impudent soldier's skull.'

Loving's voice was famous for carrying across a county or two in Texas, even in casual conversation. Tobias didn't have to repeat the message and was quickly back with a coffeepot and three cups. Loving moved a chair close to the bars and accepted a cup of coffee from Tobias.

'See, Tobias,' Loving said as he sipped the coffee. 'I always told you that Yankees can be reasonable if you treat them politely. Now, Quentin McLeod, tell me your story from the beginning.'

Oliver Loving took out a dog-eared old tally book and a short stub of a pencil, crossed his legs, touched the pencil point to his tongue, and prepared to take notes.

FIFTEEN

United States Territorial Judge Artemus Thomas Burke didn't fit many people's image of a judge. He stood well over six feet tall, weighed nearly three hundred pounds and practised blacksmithing when he had time. More than once he had restored order in a courtroom by forgetting the gavel which appeared tiny in his callused hand and slamming his fist all the way through the top of the judge's bench. He was also a former professor at William and Mary College and considered quite a legal scholar. Judge Burke would soon turn forty years old.

In a voice surprisingly high-pitched for such a huge man, he addressed the crowded courtroom in a conversational tone that put frontier people at ease but at the same time maintained a sense of dignity in the proceedings. 'We are here to hear the case of the United States of America, Territory of New Mexico, versus Quentin McLeod.'

Judge Burke removed his reading spectacles and addressed the jury. 'Mr McLeod is accused of illegal trade in firearms and human captives with the Comanches, and also with the rape of one woman, tentatively identified as

103

Mrs Carlotta Mainord. Mr McLeod has pleaded not guilty. Mr Oliver Loving from the state of Texas represents him. Mrs Brian Quitman, US Attorney for the Territory of New Mexico, will present the case against Mr McLeod. You have been instructed and sworn.'

Judge Burke's summary of the case sent McLeod's thoughts back to Carlotta. So far as he knew, she still lay in a coma, her survival in question. He closed his eyes and offered a silent prayer then realized that it was the first time he'd prayed since he stood by Jewel's grave in Florida seventeen months earlier.

Since Fort Sumner didn't have a regular courtroom, a large hall the army used for dances and saber practice had been cleared. The walls and floors were of native stone, the floor worn considerably smoother than the walls. Rough lumber had been knocked together to form benches for the crowd. The odor of resin from the recently cut lumber mingled with that of tobacco smoke and leather. The mood outside the courtroom was festive, spectators having come from as far away as Santa Fe and Las Vegas. Inside, the atmosphere was one of eager expectancy.

Judge Burke's bench was a standard issue army desk, as were the prosecution and defense tables. The jurors sat on an assortment of leather- and wooden-bottomed dining and office chairs. There were jurors dressed in business suits, rough cattle country clothing, farmers' overalls and US Army dress uniforms. All were cleanly shaven and freshly barbered.

A burly black sergeant with arms so large that they threatened to split his sleeves flanked the judge on one side and a small sergeant whose thin stripe of white hair contrasted starkly with his ebony skin on the other. The third bailiff, Deputy US Marshall Waylon Tyson, added a civilian flavor to the courtroom. In contrast to the stiff military posture of the two sergeants, the blond, blue-eyed Tyson slouched his six feet three inches in the manner of his farm youth. He looked like a lank, fuzzy-cheeked teenager, but he was considered one of the most dangerous gunfighters in the New Mexico Territory.

McLeod, dressed in new black woolen pants, a starched white shirt stretched uncomfortably tight across his shoulders and a black string tie, was still bandaged around the head. Efforts to find a coat large enough for his massive chest and shoulders had failed. His worn boots looked little better than before despite vigorous brushing and polishing.

Oliver Loving, dressed in a black suit, sat beside him. Even with his leathery face and callused hands, the tall Texan looked like a lawyer rather than a cattle driver dressed up in a lawyer's suit.

Prosecutor Brian Quitman's face was even redder than usual as he wound up his opening statement. The stocky lawyer hoped eventually to be appointed a federal judge or to run for elective office, so such a case as this wasn't to be overlooked or treated lightly.

He delivered his opening argument with the fervor of an election speech, focusing on the spectators as much as the jurors. 'Quentin McLeod is a combination of the most heinous criminal types in the New Mexico Territory. Quentin McLeod is a Comanchero who arms the vicious savages so that they can ravage the hard-working, God-fearing settlers of this frontier. He trafficks in human flesh, buying your wives, your daughters, your sisters from the savages and selling them into bondage in the bordellos of heathen Mexico.'

The prosecutor paused to wipe the sweat from his face and glare at Quentin McLeod. 'And he is the perpetrator of the most universally condemned, most scandalous, most vile and odious act, viewed as a crime against humanity and nature in the entire civilized world.' He paused then pointed dramatically toward Quentin McLeod. 'He is a rapist! His past war record as a turncoat and malingerer reveals his low character. Evidence leaves no doubt of his guilt. You will be doing God's will when you find this blackguard guilty and sentence him to hang by the neck until dead.'

Quitman moved directly in front of McLeod and glared at him from no more than three feet. His eyes turned only the slightest degree to gauge the effect of his performance on the audience as his voice rasped, 'Oh, how I wish we could impose some worse punishment!'

The jury and the audience followed his glare. McLeod sat immobile, the muscles along his jaw standing rigidly out from his face. The twelve faces in the jury reflected thinly muted fury toward the defendant. McLeod could feel their hostility even without looking.

Judge Burke waited until the muttering evoked by Quitman's oratory died down before turning toward the defense table. 'Mr Loving, would you like to make an opening statement to the jury?'

Oliver Loving took a moment to push the papers in front of him into a neat stack, then slowly straightened to his full height before responding, 'Yes, your honor.' He stepped in front of the jury but stared out the window as if looking for someone or something before finally turning his attention to the jury.

Oliver Loving had been a figure of great interest to the people of Fort Sumner ever since he and Charles Goodnight had appeared out of the deserts to the south with a herd of cattle. Every knowledgeable person *knew* cattle couldn't be driven across the arid, Comanche-controlled wastes of West Texas and southern New Mexico, but the Texans had done so anyway. Loving had helped to stop the lynching and now volunteered for what seemed the impossible task of defending Quentin McLeod in court. Every eye in the courtroom was riveted on the Texan.

Loving cleared his throat. 'Gentlemen of the jury, you have listened to my worthy opponent summarize his case very eloquently. His case is going to be built around the testimony of two witnesses, Ian Richards and Captain Thomas Madsen. Ian Richards is what we would call a hostile witness. Our Roman forebears would have called him an *anguis in herbis.*'

Loving paused and walked to stand in front of Ian Richards, seated in the front bench, and towered above him much as Quitman had over Quentin McLeod. He paused until he again had the audience holding its breath. The words rolled off his tongue in velvety resonance. '*Anguis in herbis*! Ian Richards, *anguis in herbis*!'

Richards's face turned red; he clenched his long fingers into tight fists. Loving watched his reaction and smiled. The tall Texan turned back to the jury. 'You must decide whether or not to believe this *anguis in herbis*. Remember that this alien, this British expatriate' – Loving allowed the words to hang in the air before he resumed – 'this expatriate from his own homeland, was the person found

107

in possession of the lady in question, Mrs Carlotta Mainord. We will show that, actually, Mr McLeod was Mrs Mainord's savior and protector. "*Semper Fidelis*".'

Loving's deep melodious voice reverberated off the walls as he repeated the phrases. 'Quentin McLeod, *semper fidelis*. Ian Richards, *anguis in herbis.*'

The jurors' faces gradually softened and became riveted on the Texan, entranced with the sound of the words. 'Mr McLeod in fact rescued Mrs Mainord, a widow lady, and brought her toward this very fort, despite tribulations which the Romans would have described as *semper aqua y legarti anum. Semper aqua y legarti anum.* Until' – Loving paused while every person present, even the prosecutor, hung on his words – 'until Ian Richards shot Mr McLeod and seized Mrs Mainord.' He turned and stared out the window again, then sat down. Jurors and spectators whispered.

McLeod leaned toward Loving and whispered, 'What is that *angwees* thing you called him?'

Loving tapped the edges of his papers into neat alignment then held them in such a way as to shield his face from the jurors. '*Anguis in herbis.* Means "snake in the grass".'

McLeod stared at Loving in surprise. 'Snake in— What was that long phrase? *Semper agua—*'

Loving interrupted. '*Aqua,* not *agua. Semper aqua y leqarti anum.* It's kind of a mixture of Latin and Spanish. It means "always up to your ass in water and alligators".'

'What does that have to do with anything?' McLeod asked, furrowing his brows.

'Nothing,' Loving responded and smiled. 'But people expect a good show at a trial like this one. Some jurors traveled several days to get here. It wouldn't help our case to disappoint them.'

Judge Burke rapped his gavel. 'Mr Quitman, call your first witness.'

Loving dug through his pocket and brought out his pencil stub, despite an elegant pen and ink well in front of him. The Texan touched the pencil point to his tongue and prepared to take notes on the testimony, then turned back to McLeod while holding his old tally book to block his lips. 'Don't tell my partner that I know what those Latin phrases mean. He laughs at me when he thinks I'm faking it, and Charles doesn't have much fun.'

Ian Richards made an impressive looking witness with his elegantly cut black suit, military posture and assured manner. He recounted his story – how he happened upon McLeod buying the white woman from the Comanches, rescued her and was wounded in the process. The jurors' hostility became almost a tangible, physical force.

When Loving's turn to cross-examine came, he rose slowly and again peered out the window, attracting the curiosity of spectators and jurors. At length he turned toward Ian Richards and began in his velvet drawl, 'Mr Richards, why were you on the Staked Plains in Comanche country all by yourself?'

Richards seemed surprised at the question and hesitated before answering, 'Hunting. . . .' He seemed momentarily unbalanced by Loving's raised eyebrow but quickly recovered. 'Hunting mineral deposits. I am interested in mining properties.'

Loving stood with his side to Richards and faced the jury. 'You have experience in mining properties, Mr Richards?'

Richards smiled, feeling he had an opening. 'Yes. When I served as an officer in the British Army, first in India and later in Australia.'

Loving again gazed out the window before moving closer to the jury. He turned quickly and locked eyes with Ian Richards. 'Why did you leave the British Army?'

Richards seemed perfectly at ease now as he answered, 'Wanderlust. The salary wasn't important to me.'

'Did your leaving the British Army have anything to do with your treatment of women?' Loving asked.

Richards managed a smile, but inwardly he seethed. 'Of course not.'

Loving stared at Richards until the Englishman turned his eyes away. 'Mr Richards, are you telling us that you, an experienced mining man, went looking for mineral deposits on the Staked Plains, which are alluvial in nature, when there is so much country nearby which is volcanic in origin?'

The Texan now had the rapt attention of everyone present. Almost everyone in New Mexico Territory was interested in minerals. Every cowboy riding herd, every muleskinner driving freight wagons and every housewife hanging out clothes had one eye out for signs of gold or silver, hoping to find the next bonanza. Even those who couldn't read or write knew that one almost never found gold or silver on an alluvial plain. Ian Richards's statement didn't ring true at all.

Richards looked down; his voice trailed slightly. 'I was crossing the Staked Plains to get to the Canadian River canyons.'

Loving arched his brows and smiled. 'Quite interesting. No more questions.'

Jurors and spectators gazed speculatively at Ian Richards, obviously weighing the exchange.

The prosecution next called Captain Madsen, who looked resplendent in full dress uniform. He proceeded to give a low-down picture of the 'Galvanized Yankees' he had commanded on the plains during the late war and pictured McLeod as the worst of a bad lot.

Oliver Loving gazed out the windows rather than look toward the officer. Many jurors paid more attention to Loving than Madsen. 'Lieutenant Madsen—' Loving began.

'Captain! Captain Madsen!' Madsen practically shouted, his face red.

'My apologies, Captain.' Loving turned to the jurors and gallery, smiling as if they were all sharing in a joke. 'I always had trouble with Yankee ranks. You say that the ex-Confederates you commanded were not very good soldiers?'

'Terrible. Worst I ever commanded,' Madsen responded pompously. 'Little discipline or military bearing. Most unmilitary.'

'Would you say, Captain,' Oliver Loving asked, his drawl more elongated than usual, 'that the Confederates were most unmilitary at Perryville, Lookout Mountain, Shiloh, Chickamauga?'

'They fought very well in each,' Madsen grudgingly admitted. After all, there were several southerners on the jury.

Loving now stood close and glared down at Madsen. 'Are you aware, Captain Madsen that Quentin McLeod – Sergeant Quentin McLeod – fought in each of these?'

'No, I—'

111

'Why were you out on the plains when the big war was going on back East, Captain Madsen? Seems a strange place for a West Point graduate to have been.'

Madsen's face darkened to an even deeper red as he snapped back angrily, 'Fighting the savages, especially with inferior troops, called for bold, decisive leaders.'

'Yes. I suppose that's why Ulysses Grant, Tecumseh Sherman and Phil Sheridan didn't qualify to spend the war in the West.' The softness of Oliver Loving's voice underscored his sarcasm.

The crowd tittered. Loving paused and walked to where he could peer out the window again. Then he took a sheet of paper from beside McLeod at the table and returned his attention to Captain Madsen. 'Where did you rank in your class at West Point, Captain?'

Madsen hesitated a long moment. 'Mr Loving, discussing one's class rank is considered to be poor form among graduates of—'

'Captain Madsen,' Loving interrupted, 'where in the class?'

Madsen looked on the verge of explosion but answered as if trying to explain something to someone who didn't have the background to understand. 'There are a number of categories, Mr Loving. Each cadet is ranked in each of those categories.'

Loving unfolded the piece of paper in his hand and held it up. 'Your overall ranking, Captain? If I pointed to your name on a list of class rankings, would it be up here near the top?' He pointed to the top of the page, paused then slid his hand slowly toward the bottom. Every eye in the room followed Loving's finger. 'Or would it be down near the bottom?'

Madsen glared at Loving but didn't answer.

Loving took a pair of reading spectacles from his vest pocket and placed them on his nose. 'Would you like me to start at the top of the list and read until I find your name?'

Madsen sat silently until Loving used his big finger to push his glasses up to the bridge of his nose. Madsen cleared his throat and answered through tightly clenched teeth, 'Second to last.'

Loving looked to the jury and audience drawing them in. 'I beg your pardon, Captain?'

'Second to last,' Madsen answered, his eyes drifting toward the floor.

Loving feigned surprise and leaned forward as if listening intently. 'Would you speak louder? I want the jury to hear.'

'Second to last.'

'Next to last, Captain?' Loving leaned over Madsen and glared down at him. 'Isn't it true that you were sent to the plains because you were a reject? Expendable? No good? Isn't it true that your career was a failure and that you were bitter? You took it out on the Galvanized Yankees and would like to get rid of Quentin McLeod any way you can so that people here won't find out what a small-caliber tinhorn you are?'

Quitman leaped to his feet. 'Objection! Your honor, Mr Loving is completely out of order!'

Judge Burke slammed his fist on the desk to quiet the courtroom. 'Mr Loving, you are quite out of order. The court will not allow the fact that you are not an attorney to excuse such behavior.'

Loving, now standing behind the defense table bowed

slightly and spoke in his most velvety drawl, 'My apologies to the court. Of course, the jury should forget my remarks.' He sat down and placed the paper he had held in his hand on top of the others.

McLeod opened it. It was blank. Loving leaned toward McLeod and whispered, 'Stonewall Jackson ranked dead last in his class in tactics.'

The prosecution called Doctor Joseph Carpenter who confirmed that he had been present when Carlotta and Richards had come upon the cavalry patrol and when McLeod had arrived. After Doctor Carpenter described his examination of all three, the prosecutor came to the part the crowd eagerly awaited.

'In your judgment, had this woman been . . . violated?'

'Yes,' the doctor answered evenly.

Jurors and spectators muttered angrily yet leaned forward to catch every word.

'What makes you think that?' the prosecutor asked.

Doctor Carpenter hesitated then answered as if carefully choosing his words, 'Physical evidence was consistent with a very brutal violation.'

The jury and spectators muttered angrily. McLeod felt a sinking in the pit of his stomach. Quitman gloated as he sat down.

McLeod felt as if the noose was already tightening around his neck. Rather than pay attention to Loving's questioning of Doctor Carpenter, he began to search his brain for a way to escape. His mind raced desperately, but every idea was a dead end. Suddenly, the trial seemed an empty form, a meaningless and cruel game to be played out, like a mouse being toyed with by a cat.

While McLeod's mind raced, the jury and spectators

waited eagerly to see if Loving would try to brow beat the doctor as he had Captain Madsen. Almost everyone in New Mexico Territory knew what a tough codger Doctor Joseph Carpenter was, despite his diminutive size and soft voice.

'In your opinion, Doctor Carpenter,' Loving asked the doctor, deference in his voice, 'your opinion, as one of the most respected physicians in New Mexico, a physician to whose expertise some in this room, some on this jury, owe their very lives – in your opinion did the physical damage from the crime appear to be less than twenty-four hours old?'

'In my opinion, yes,' the doctor answered confidently, looking directly at the jurors.

After a moment of silence, muttering spread through the room. Judge Burke allowed the noise to run its course and then diminish.

'On what do you base that judgment, Doctor?' Loving asked, easing to the side so that Doctor Carpenter was the focus of the jurors' attention rather than himself.

The doctor responded with his voice still even and comfortable, his eyes fixed on the jurors. 'I base my judgment on the conditions of the physical trauma, such as the degree to which bruises had discolored and swollen, abrasions had reddened and the degree and time required for these symptoms to continue to worsen, then lessen, during further treatment.'

Eyes shifted from Doctor Carpenter to Ian Richards. The Englishman sat with his eyes straight ahead, motionless except for clenching and unclenching his fingers.

Loving towered over Richards as he continued, 'Ian

Richards testified that he rescued the lady in question two days before he made contact with you. That's forty-eight hours. Does that agree with what he told Major Byrd upon your juncture?'

'Yes.'

'So if Ian Richards is telling the truth about how long Mrs Mainord had been with him, the attack would have taken place while she was with him?'

Doctor Carpenter paused for a moment then responded, 'In my opinion, the brutal attack took place in the last twenty-four hours or less before I first examined her.'

'Thank you,' Loving told the witness and sat down by McLeod.

McLeod grasped Loving's arm and whispered in his ear, 'Get me a gun!'

'What?' Loving asked, his usually unflappable demeanor shaken.

'A gun,' McLeod whispered. 'Get me a gun.'

Loving held a sheaf of papers to block his and McLeod's lips, although the jury and spectators were intent on the prosecutor's approach to question the doctor again.

'They're going to hang me,' McLeod whispered urgently.

'No. Believe me, they won't,' Loving answered.

McLeod managed to brush Loving's hip as he shifted his left hand to the side of his chair, as if acquiescing. There was no gun there. Quickly McLeod swept the courtroom with his eyes. No one had guns showing except the two sergeants serving as bailiffs and Deputy Marshall Waylon Tyson.

McLeod plotted his move. He would take one step to clear the corner of the desk in front of him. On the third step, he would plant his left foot in front of Tyson. Plant the foot, roll the hip, drive a hard right to the marshal's belly, grab his pistol with his left hand, two more steps and out the open window. The sergeants would never get their pistols from their flap-covered holsters. No one would expect such a move, he hoped.

But his left hand and arm were still working poorly. Could he move them quickly and accurately? And what would he find outside? He racked his memory, trying to remember what he had noticed about that side of the building. *Nothing.*

His chance was poor, McLeod knew, but it was more chance than offered by a hanging. As if reading his mind, Loving leaned over again and whispered, 'It's going to be all right. Trust me.'

McLeod redirected his thinking. Loving would never make such a blanket statement unless he knew something, McLeod told himself. How could the Texan be so sure?

The window! Loving staring out the window before and after questioning witnesses. McLeod had thought this to be a piece of histrionics to entertain the jury and divert their attention from the damaging testimony of the prosecution, but there must be another reason. McLeod again swept the room with his eyes. Only Tobias Wilcox was present from the Texas cattle crew. Goodnight and his tough herders must be absent for some reason.

Rescue! They must plan to take him by force if the trial went against him, McLeod decided. His hopes soared then plummeted even more deeply. If he and the Texans fled, what would happen to Carlotta? Who would know to protect her from Ian Richards? McLeod's mind was in more of a whirl than ever.

He tried to direct his attention to the prosecutor, who was again questioning Doctor Carpenter, but schemes for escape and concern for Carlotta drowned him out in McLeod's mind. The jurors, on the other hand, paid rapt attention.

'Is it possible that other doctors might disagree with your opinion about the twenty-four hours?' Quitman asked.

'You could find some doctor to disagree about almost anything,' Doctor Carpenter allowed.

'You had never treated the lady before, had you, Doctor?'

'No.'

'Would it be accurate to say,' Quitman asked, 'that bruises would discolor, swell, physically change in response to injury at different rates in different persons?'

'Yes,' the doctor answered.

'Then your conclusion as to how long it would take this particular individual to discolor, swell, react in whatever manner, might be regarded as supposition rather than hard, medical fact?'

Doctor Carpenter hesitated, then responded, 'It is my judgment.'

Now it was Oliver Loving's chance to call witnesses. He called Ethan Thompson. A murmur spread through the courtroom as the old mule skinner and livery operator strode forward in gray dress trousers, a long, black dress coat with swallowtails, a stiffly starched white shirt, and a black tie. Only his scuffed boots looked familiar. No one in Fort Sumner had ever seen him in a coat and tie.

While Ethan was sworn in, Loving stared out the window again. Eventually the Texan turned and winked at McLeod. McLeod's eyes swept the room again, certain that the room would soon explode into action. He slid his chair a few inches to give himself better clearance for quick movement. Taking Waylon Tyson must still be his first move, McLeod decided.

He looked into Tyson's cool, blue eyes and felt chill. Tyson was reputed to be one of the deadliest men in the Territory, but McLeod saw no other choice. He stretched his legs to loosen the muscles then set his feet underneath him for quick movement. He opened and closed his left hand, wishing desperately he had worked harder to regain better use of it. Gingerly he bent and straightened his left arm several times. It worked fairly smoothly but hadn't nearly regained all of its strength. He returned his attention to Oliver Loving and watched for some indication of when to act.

Loving turned back to Judge Burke. 'Your honor, instead of questioning Ethan Thompson, I'd like to call' – he paused and looked expectantly toward the courtroom door. All eyes followed his. The door handle turned – 'Carlotta Mainord.'

Señora Baeza came in holding Carlotta by one elbow; Charles Goodnight helped support her by the other. Two more of the Texans flanked them with shotguns.

McLeod stood in stunned silence. People scrambled for a better view.

Ian Richards took advantage of the ruckus to leap out a window.

SIXTEEN

Archibald McNabb could get no breath to scream. His jagged yellow teeth stood out against his snowy beard and mustache. His crutches lay flung to the side. The black-clad apparition that had hurtled from the window of the courtroom on to McNabb rolled quickly to his feet. His pallid face was so distorted that the knot of startled people standing around McNabb took a moment to recognize Ian Richards. The tall Englishman's long fingers slapped to his hip then started to the back of his neck. He stopped.

'He's escaped!' Ian Richards gasped breathlessly. 'Waylon Tyson and the Texans are breaking McLeod free. Shoot them on sight!'

Richards turned and dashed away. 'Watch out!'

The bystanders looked up just in time to see Deputy Marshal Waylon Tyson sail out of the window. The lithe marshal landed lightly on the balls of his feet, surprised into inaction when he saw several people clawing at waist bands for pistols. He held up his empty hands to calm them.

A big, red-faced man in a worn, black suit dug ineffectively for a small ball-and-cap revolver in his waist band. 'Shoot the bastard!'

'Ian Richards—' the marshal began, then buckled to the ground grasping his groin. Archibald McNabb raised his heavy oak crutch and swung down on the marshal's head for a second hit.

'There's McLeod!' someone yelled.

The crowd gathered around Tyson rushed away, leaving only Archibald McNabb with the marshal. The old freighter lay his crutch down and leveled an old Navy Colt on Tyson.

Ian Richards sprinted to the nearest alley as if headed to Thompson's stable, but once out of sight of the courtroom, he circled back in the opposite direction. Two army privates stepped away from the wall, thinking they had been caught lax on duty. 'Quick!' Richards snapped authoritatively. 'Quentin McLeod has escaped. Help find him. Shoot him on sight!'

The soldiers hurried off. Ian Richards was surprised to find Sergeant Joshua Everett inside the jail but reacted quickly. 'Sergeant! The prisoner has escaped. All hands to the courtroom,' he barked as if he had never left the British Army.

The sergeant grabbed a rifle and cartridge belt then stopped in shock staring out the window at the sight of Quentin McLeod hugging Carlotta Mainord amidst a crowd that seemed to be wishing them well. They were obviously not being chased.

He whirled back towards Richards. Understanding registered for the briefest moment before he sagged to the floor, his throat slashed. 'Tough luck, old chap,' Richards said sarcastically as he wiped his knife blade clean on the sergeant's shirt.

Richards took the sergeant's rifle and ammunition belt, then stuck his pistol under his belt. Quickly and efficiently he opened a labeled drawer, took a packet of pistol cartridges and placed them in the side pocket of his coat. The Englishman took the sergeant of the guard's canteen, another sitting on the shelf, an empty coffee pot, and a cloth bag of coffee beans. He stuffed them in a pair of saddle-bags conveniently nearby and headed out the back door. Outside, Richards quickly looked in both directions, mounted one of the cavalry horses and led the other two away with him.

He turned the horses behind a thick screen of mesquite and into a dry wash heading roughly in the direction of his ranch and rode away quickly, but not at such a pace to raise a dust.

In the jail, Captain Madsen warily stepped out of the adjoining storage closet where he had cowered while Richards had been there. The captain lowered the hammer on his pistol and sat down unsteadily. He avoided looking at the body of Sergeant Everett as he uncorked the bottle for which he had gone to the office before Richards arrived there. With both hands he tilted it and took a long drink. He eased warily around Sergeant Everett's body, slipped out the back door, looked to see that no one was around and hurried down the back alley to Ethan Thompson's livery stable. There he was calmly currying his horse when Ethan Thompson rushed into the stable.

The old livery operator was surprised to find Captain Madsen present. Thompson had long felt contempt for the captain, because he took no care of his animals and didn't require his soldiers to do so either. He knew that there was no more certain sign of incompetence in a cavalry officer. Nevertheless, Madsen was the only audience he had, so he blurted out the news. 'Ian Richards was the real Comanchero. He's escaped. The major wants all troops assembled.'

The words had barely escaped his mouth before a bugle sounded to signal all soldiers to stations. Captain Madsen didn't seem very surprised by the news or the bugle call, Thompson noticed.

'Saddle up for me and bring my horse to the post,' Madsen ordered in a condescending voice.

'Saddle your own horse,' the old man snapped back and left.

Captain Madsen had a sinking feeling that this was the kind of treatment he could expect from everyone in Fort Sumner after the manner in which Oliver Loving had humiliated him in court.

SEVENTEEN

The world seemed a giant, confused whirlwind to Carlotta. With each step she felt as if she was stepping into a hole and was surprised every time her foot landed upon solid ground. Walls and doors and the ground seemed to tilt at crazy angles. She vaguely remembered protesting when Charles Goodnight and Señora Baeza had urged her to stay in bed rather than go to McLeod.

Everything grew even more confused when she had stepped into the courtroom. Everyone stopped and stared. McLeod stood. The rest of the room faded away and ceased to exist for her. She had feared that Señora Baeza and Goodnight had been lying when they told her that McLeod had survived the battle with the Comanches.

Everyone yelled and struggled to get by her and rush outside. Only Goodnight's arms kept her upright as men shouldered by. Was this another dream? She was still uncertain of what was dream and what was real. She clearly remembered the shootout with the Comanches until her memory stopped abruptly in the middle of the battle. She remembered snatches of waking up while lying across the pommel of a saddle. She remembered a brief image of grass and legs of a horse, but from the wrong angles. And it seemed as if cold fingers had touched her as she bounced along in pain. By the campfire, other vague images.

Quentin McLeod followed the eyes of everyone in the courtroom. There stood Carlotta alive and even more beautiful than he had remembered. Despite a bandage around her head she stood with the proud, defiant carriage he so admired. He tried to rush to her but found himself rooted to the floor.

He screamed as he saw Carlotta buckle under the rush of bodies toward the door, but even he couldn't hear his own voice over the roar of the crowd. He pushed, pulled and knocked bodies in every direction. He struggled to reach Carlotta, who was now completely out of his sight. He felt the same kind of panic he had felt when pulled from his cell by the lynch mob. He couldn't see her anywhere. It was as if he had seen an apparition, there for a moment then vanished.

Goodnight and some of his Texans clustered around her and rushed her outside, away from the jostling of the crowd. She kept trying to turn back to find McLeod again but was practically carried by those who surrounded her. Every part of her body hurt. Men shouted orders. It seemed that hundreds talked at once. So many unfamiliar faces stared at her as if she were some sort of curiosity.

Through the courtroom door, McLeod saw the bright emerald-green dress and the white bandages. It seemed that everything moved maddeningly slowly as he struggled to get through the crush of bodies to her. At last he was there. He enveloped her, pulling her tightly to his chest, glorying in her warmth. The smell of her freshly washed hair almost overpowered him, taking him back to their embrace the last night together in the brakes of the Canadian River. There were many things he had hoped to have the opportunity to tell her, but now he was unable to speak.

Carlotta could feel and smell him. He was real! He was alive! The rest of the crowd faded away for her. She felt him wince as her chin dug into his shoulder and became aware that her chin was pressing against tightly wrapped cloth bandages. She pushed herself away, struggling to separate lest she aggravate his injury, but he held tight. 'No,' she protested. It seemed she could smell warm blood on his shoulder. She struggled to push away so she could see if he was really all right.

At last McLeod loosened his hold and held her at arm's length, looked at her as if he had never seen her before. Carlotta suddenly realized how she must look. She hadn't really looked in a mirror when Señora Baeza helped her dress. Her hand went to her head and felt the bandage and, around the edge of it, the prickly bristles of the first growth of new hair. The right side of her face was swollen.

Voices from the crowd became distinct. 'My God! Look at McLeod's scalp,' one said. Carlotta stiffened in anger. She wanted to find the speaker and lash out at him, but faces and voices were too mingled. Then it was a woman's voice. 'Somehow I don't think a decent woman would have survived what was supposed to have happened to her.'

'Look how they carry on,' another voice added. 'And

they were together alone out there.'

McLeod pushed himself away, horrified. He looked at her, hoping desperately she hadn't heard. He began to separate himself from her. Women, he knew, set a great deal of store in appearances. It wasn't fair to her.

She felt McLeod's hands go from soft to board rigid. His lips twisted. He looked at her as if horrified. Carlotta felt as if she had been dipped in ice. His hands still rested on her shoulders but were now cold. The hands that had drawn her so close were now holding her away at arm's length. His eyes looked as if he were seeing her for the first time.

'I'm soiled goods,' she thought. That must be the reason for the horror on his face. The stiff resolve that had steeled her to walk to the courtroom melted. The crowd around her began to spin.

McLeod moved quickly to catch her and closed his arms tightly back around her and lifted. For a brief moment she luxuriated in the warmth of his presence. But then she saw his face twisted in distaste, as if holding something unclean. Fury surged through her. She shrugged free and pushed his arms away. 'No!' she told him, her voice harsher than intended. She looked for a familiar face and settled on a small man with a black medical bag. Vaguely she remembered him bent over her, bathing, wrapping, examining. She reached her arm toward him. 'Doctor, get me away, please.'

She was irritated to hear the pleading tone in her voice. She was Carlotta Castro Mainord. Her mother died fighting Comanches. She herself had fought and survived. An image of her mother standing straight, thumbing back the hammer of the big Colt, fierce defiance on her face came to Carlotta and steeled her. She stood erect with her head up, defiance in the eyes that swept over the crowd. Señora Baeza took one elbow and Doctor Carpenter the other. She leaned heavily on both but walked with her head erect.

'No,' she admonished herself as she fought back the tears of rage and humiliation. 'No more tears. No matter what.'

McLeod felt as if a dagger had been thrust into his innards. How could he hope she would care for such a scarred and tarnished man, now that she no longer needed him? His mind involuntarily flashed back to their warm embraces the last night in the canyon. But now she was obviously repulsed by him. Anger flared when he saw her turn and look for a way to get away from him. He refused the impulse to follow when Doctor Carpenter led her toward his buggy, but strong hands forced McLeod along with them. Doctor Carpenter urged him to get into the buggy. McLeod looked at Carlotta and turned his face away, shook his head. 'No!' he said emphatically.

Carlotta's face burned with humiliation and anger.

A different hand took him by the arm. He tried to resist, but Charles Goodnight didn't relent. McLeod didn't want to humiliate Carlotta by his presence, and he didn't want to force his company on someone who didn't want it. 'You need the doctor,' Goodnight told him in his brusque manner. 'You've already proven you don't have much judgment by letting Oliver represent you in court.'

Carlotta moved to the side of the buggy seat to make room for McLeod, but her expression made clear her displeasure at his presence. 'No!' McLeod told Goodnight as he resisted getting into the buggy. But the Texan wasn't accustomed to taking no for an answer, and McLeod was in no condition to resist. He sat beside Carlotta. She kept her face turned away.

They rode away in mutual silence.

EIGHTEEN

Ian Richards sat motionless on the side of a hill overlooking his ranch, looking and listening for any unusual activity, his location screened by young sycamores. Despite the late season the range held a tint of green, the result of an unusually wet year and warm autumn.

Only the raucous chorus of crows cawing over his alfalfa field broke the silence. Four pronghorns grazing in an unworried manner along the main trail to Fort Sumner provided a good indication that no one was approaching from that direction. Richards's memory returned to the times Ethan Thompson had shown up out of seemingly thin air and felt unease ooze through him. He hated the old man. He wanted badly to wait and watch longer but expected that his ranch would be searched soon. The fugitive took one last look in the direction of town, saw nothing and walked his horse toward his ranch, keeping the big barn between him and town.

He sat outside the barn and listened again but neither heard nor saw anything out of the way. For a moment the Englishman enjoyed the warmth of the New Mexico sun soaking into his black coat, then dismounted and eased through a small door in the side of the barn. Smoothly and quietly he eased inside, keeping his back to the wall. His long fingers opened and closed nervously around the big Colt Army Issue revolver. The click when he cocked the hammer sounded as loud as thunder to him.

The usual smells of fresh hay, dried manure, leather tack and horse sweat greeted his nostrils. Nothing seemed out of order, but the fugitive felt prickles up and down his back. He had survived more than once because he had paid attention to such sensations. His gut tightened. There was a slight movement to his left, barely visible.

Ian Richards dropped to his right knee and rolled once to his right. Something white flashed. He came up in a firing position, scrambling desperately to find the white again. A glimpse of the white to his right and behind froze him. As an experienced fighting man, he knew when he had no chance. He raised his arms carefully above his head, secure in the feeling that the fools representing the law wouldn't shoot him when they had the best chance. He spoke calmly and carefully so the person wouldn't mistake his move. 'I'm going to turn to my right to face you. I'm putting the hammer down and dropping the gun.'

He took a deep breath to slow his racing heart and fought hard for control. Carefully he eased the hammer down on his Colt and dropped the big army pistol on to the hay litter below. He waited for what seemed a long time, his muscles tensing more each second. The silence baffled him. Very slowly he turned to see who his captor was.

A white cat sat staring at him, its big eyes quite puzzled by the whole process. 'Well I'll be damned!' The

Comanchero laughed softly to himself and picked the Colt up again. He smiled and extended his left hand toward the cat. The cat stretched his neck to sniff then rubbed against the proffered hand.

Like a flash, the long fingers grabbed the cat's head and pinned it to the bale of hay. The pistol barrel slashed downward. The cat made no sound. It lay, eyes open, the back of its skull smashed into the bale of hay. Blood oozed from its mouth. Richards spoke to himself while he slipped the pistol back under his belt. 'Damn cats. I hate them.'

'Freeze, Mr Cat Killer.' A deep voice said, 'I thought you had me when I scared that cat. Put your hands on top of your head and turn around real slow.'

Richards was in near total shock now. Carefully he did just as told. The huge black sergeant who had been one of the bailiffs in the trial pointed a businesslike Spencer repeater at his belly. The .54 caliber bore looked as big to Richards as the maw of Palo Duro Canyon.

The sergeant smiled, but neither his eyes nor the Spencer wavered. 'Good thing I'm not a white cat.'

Ian Richards didn't move or change expression. Instead his eyes remained locked directly on those of the buffalo soldier. The sergeant licked his lips. 'Now take your left hand and ease that other Colt out of your belt. Use your left thumb and one finger. Real careful like.' The sergeant chuckled again. 'I figgered you'd have something stashed here. This ought to be good for some kind of reward.'

Richards grasped the Colt with thumb and forefinger, his other fingers widely spread. He removed the Colt as gently as if handling the most fragile china cup. His eyes remained locked with those of the sergeant.

'Now drop it gently, just like you did for that cat.' The sergeant laughed his deep, rumbling laugh. 'Drop it for this black cat like you did for that white cat.'

Richards smiled, eye-to-eye with the sergeant, never wavering. Now that he knew exactly what situation he faced, calm suffused every fiber of his body. He smiled slightly. The sergeant swallowed nervously at the smile. Richards tossed the Colt to his left rather than dropping it. The sergeant glanced briefly toward where the Colt landed on the floor. It bounced once then lay still in the soft litter of the hay.

He looked back just in time to see a small but wicked dagger hurtling toward him. The dagger plunged to its hilt, cutting through the left eye to the brain. The sergeant's hands never even grabbed at the dagger; he dropped to the floor like a sack of feed.

Ian Richards stepped forward and rotated the blade roughly as he yanked it free. He kneeled, cut, and ripped off the scalp as quickly as any Comanche could have done. 'Comanches like woolly scalps, buffalo soldier.' His laugh was an evil parody of the sergeant's laugh.

The Comanchero wiped his dagger blade clean, slipped it into a holster behind his neck and stepped quickly toward the tack room for his cache of supplies.

NINETEEN

McLeod had longed for Carlotta dozens of times every day but now rode painfully silent and disappointed, searching his brain futilely, trying to think of something, anything, to say. He felt as awkward and helpless as a teenage boy with his first romance. Even the joy of being free in the afternoon sun after confinement in the jail was lost to him. Doctor Carpenter gave up on attempts to make conversation as they came within sight of Ian Richards's ranch.

McLeod snapped upright when he saw soldiers rushing around there, their rifles at the ready. The corporal in charge of the detail assigned to guard Carlotta and McLeod spurred his horse forward to confer with a sergeant-major overseeing the search then held up his hand to halt the buggy.

'It must be him. I'm going,' McLeod said and climbed down from the buggy.

Carlotta reached to stop him but was too late. He strode toward the house, but soon began to weave and stagger. One of the soldiers spurred his mount forward and caught McLeod by the collar of his shirt as he sagged. Carlotta remained frozen, half-standing as McLeod clutched the soldier's saddle to keep from falling.

'That's either the stubbornest man or the stupidest man you have,' the doctor said and shook his head in exasperation. He glanced over his shoulder at Carlotta. 'But you seem to be a pretty good match,' he added with frustration evident is his voice.

'He's been dead no more than an hour, probably less,' Doctor Carpenter told Waylon Tyson and Major Byrd as he pulled a gray army blanket over the sergeant's body, then wiped his hands on a feed sack lying nearby. He glanced back at the dead cat and the scalped body and continued, 'Major, it's not my place to tell you your business, but this man is going to come back and try to kill Mrs Mainord.'

'You think he might come back here?' the major asked skeptically.

'I'm telling you that he *will* be back here.'

'Mrs Mainord is going to need you more than ever in the next few days,' Doctor Carpenter told Señora Baeza. He opened his medical bag. 'I want you to have this. Do you know how to use it?'

Her eyes grew large as she took the short-barreled revolver the doctor handed her. She nodded and looked in a questioning manner toward Quentin McLeod's room.

'Not for Mr McLeod, señora,' he assured her and smiled. 'In my medical opinion they won't need your chaperonage to remain chaste for the next couple of weeks.' The doctor's demeanor turned serious again. 'I've told Major Byrd that Ian Richards will come back for Mrs Mainord. The major is going to increase the guard details, but Richards is a very resourceful man, and I don't think the soldiers really believe he's going to return.' He paused and looked at her meaningfully. 'He won't expect this from you.'

Señora Baeza hefted the gun knowingly, checked its balance by dropping it into a line to sight then made sure the percussion caps were in place. She pointed it at imaginary targets, smoothly and confidently, then looked up at the doctor and nodded her satisfaction and approval. 'For Ian Richards, Doctor, but also' – she paused and pointed her head toward Quentin McLeod's room – 'if needed.'

Doctor Carpenter couldn't hide his surprise. She looked serious for a moment then chuckled heartily at her own joke and tucked the pistol out of sight in her voluminous clothing.

Doctor Carpenter walked to his buggy, set his bag under the seat and settled in. He sat motionless for a moment, obviously in thought then spoke aloud to himself. 'Well, I'll be damned.' He laughed softly to himself. Then he became serious again. He reached under the rim of the driver's seat and pulled out a short, double-barreled shotgun, checked the loads and returned it to its hiding place.

TWENTY

Patience didn't come naturally to Ian Richards. Outwaiting Comanches was one of the toughest challenges he ever faced in dealing with them. The tall Englishman leaned back against the rock and blew across his metal cup to cool his coffee. The Comanches were being more cautious than usual. Perhaps they had heard what had happened to Thundercloud's raiding party. The four had been hiding in the brush and watched him for at least an hour.

Ian Richards tried to concentrate on his surroundings rather than think of the Comanches. His experiences had convinced him that the natives were very sensitive to a person's thoughts. He concentrated on the afternoon breeze in the canyon created by the downward flow of cooling air. Boughs in the nearby plum thicket rattled in the breeze. He wondered where the bees that buzzed past him would be feeding this time of the year. The Comanches called honeybees 'White man's flies,' he remembered. *Such primitives.* He watched the passage of a cloud's shadow from the north to the south rim of the canyon.

Richards emerged from his reverie and smiled to himself. One of the four Comanches emerged from a mesquite thicket on horseback and rode toward the Comanchero's fire. Richards let the rider approach to thirty feet without acknowledging his presence. Eventually, without looking directly at the approaching rider, he took his extra coffee cup, filled it and sat it on a rock next to a small sack of sugar.

The rider was a swarthy, middle-aged man with the stocky, short-legged body so typical of the Comanches. Even from a distance a hand-sized burn scar was apparent on the left side of his face. If Richards's observations were correct, the three left in the brush should be a woman and two children. Richards tried to remember the name of the warrior. Richards had traded with him in the past, but not frequently.

The Comanche sat on his horse silently for a long minute staring into Richards's eyes. Then he held up his right hand, palm forward. The Englishman hesitated for a moment before answering in the tongue of The People. 'Welcome, Horse Killer.' The name came to Richards at the last moment. 'I have only dried beef to eat, but the coffee is hot.'

Horse Killer didn't speak. The warrior carefully swept the area with his eyes once again then waved the other Comanches into Richards's camp. He slid off his horse, took the coffee and dipped liberally into the sugar. Three other riders emerged from the brush, Horse Killer's woman, a daughter, about twelve or thirteen, Richards guessed and a boy several years younger.

Richards's eyes lingered on the girl. Her large, dark eyes reminded him of New Orleans many years earlier.

The Englishman's long fingers clenched and unclenched around the now forgotten cup. His lips formed a word strange to the Comanches. 'Juliette . . . oh, Juliette.'

TWENTY-ONE

Even a dozen candles on the table failed to lighten the atmosphere. The three sat quietly at the massive, dark mahogany table in Ian Richards's dining-room. An army private cleared away the last plates and returned with a silver pot of coffee. Señora Baeza shook her head in wonder. The conversation between the two became more strained every day. It was obvious to her that each loved the other, yet they distanced themselves further each day. At times she was tempted to shake both of them, but that would be acting too much like an Anglo.

The quarters of the commanding officer of the US Army detachment at Fort Sumner would have been unimpressive in most settings, but the four-room stone house was the most grandiose dwelling near the fort. The flame in the glass chimneys of the two lanterns danced as a brisk breeze blew through the open windows. The curtains, made from plain white cotton, stood flapping out from the wall.

'There's no way he's within two hundred miles of the fort,' Major Byrd told the two Texans and Waylon Tyson as he poured rye whiskey. 'We've turned over every rock and every blade of grass. He's either near Mexico or headed to California.'

'Or he's holed up somewhere nearby making no tracks,' Waylon Tyson suggested softly.

'I can't buy that, Waylon,' the major answered as he tapped the ash from his cigar.

Oliver Loving had been uncharacteristically quiet. The tall Texan held the glass of rye between his eyes and the lantern, rolling it in his fingers, appreciating the highlights of red and amber. 'There's a simple way to find out,' he said.

Charles Goodnight looked at his partner, presuming he was about to propose something outrageous.

'What might that be?' Major Byrd asked.

Loving played with the glass of rye and lantern light for another moment and then downed the rye in one long, appreciative swallow. 'Fine liquor. Almost good enough to have been made in Tennessee or Texas,' he said. He locked his gaze on to those of the major. 'The way to know for certain is to use some of your Navajos as trackers.'

Major Byrd poured another drink for Loving before answering, 'We'll never use natives as auxiliaries in the South-west. You could never trust them.'

'I'll be damned, Oliver,' Goodnight told his partner. 'Every once in a while you come up with an idea that's not so crazy.'

'You could never trust them,' the major repeated.

'They'd do almost anything to get free of this post for a while,' Tyson argued. 'If they give their word to come back, they will.'

*

141

Captain Sterling Johnson was neither tall nor lean and had given up years earlier trying to look like a parade ground soldier, a goal no amount of spit and polish could accomplish. He shifted his position and leaned forward and announced, 'I am going to lead another expedition to look for Ian Richards. We've found no sign at all and conventional wisdom says that he is well on his way to Mexico or California by now. On the other hand, Doctor Carpenter insists that he will hide in the area and—' Captain Johnson hesitated, searching for the right way to continue.

'—and come back for me,' Carlotta completed the sentence for him.

Captain Johnson was obviously uncomfortable discussing the possibility with Carlotta. She held her crossed arms against her stomach. Her eyes flashed. 'Which do you think, Captain?'

Johnson straightened the coffee cup in its saucer and appeared to listen to the owl in the cottonwoods by the creek. At last he turned his eyes directly to Carlotta and answered, 'I'm afraid that I agree with Doctor Carpenter, Mrs Mainord. My patrol is going to search along the Canadian River. Another patrol will be working the area between here and the Sangre de Cristo Mountains. Navajo trackers will accompany both groups.'

'When do you leave?' Quentin McLeod asked.

'At first light tomorrow.'

'I'm going with you,' McLeod said and started toward the door.

'I'm afraid that's impossible, Mr McLeod,' the captain said, surprise showing both on his face and in his voice.

'I'm going,' McLeod repeated.

Johnson's face reddened. 'That's ridiculous, Mr McLeod. You're in no condition. We will be moving hard and fast as long as we have enough daylight to track each day.'

'I know his ways better than any of you. I'm going,' McLeod answered resolutely.

'I forbid it,' Captain Johnson snapped.

McLeod leaned toward the captain. 'I'm not a soldier anymore, Captain. You can't order me.'

'We won't hold back,' Captain Johnson replied sternly. 'If you don't keep up, we'll leave you.'

'Is that a promise, Captain?'

'Absolutely.'

'Great. We have a deal,' McLeod told the captain.

Johnson shook his head as he picked up his hat. 'Daylight – at the fort.'

'Don't do this,' Carlotta said hesitantly. She didn't mean to sound so distant, so she added, 'You won't be safe.'

They had talked so easily on the plains, but now McLeod couldn't find any of the right words. 'I have to go,' he finally answered without looking directly at her.

'You don't have to go kill yourself,' Carlotta snapped. 'I'll stay away from you.'

McLeod could think of nothing else to say, so he concentrated on his packing.

'You big, ugly, pigheaded . . . I hope some Comanche takes the rest of your scalp!' Carlotta exploded and stormed out.

McLeod was more confused than ever, but he understood one thing – Ian Richards had to be stopped.

143

TWENTY-TWO

'But Major, I am second in command, much senior to Captain Johnson. I protest being passed over,' Madsen almost shouted at Major Byrd.

'No,' Major Byrd, responded, not even looking up from his paperwork.

'This is most irregular. I—'

'Enough!' The major said and slammed his fist on his desk. 'The orders stand. Use your wind and your time to get your men's horses and equipment in order. Don't bother me again.'

Madsen's face flushed deeper. He snapped to attention. 'Yes sir.' Madsen saluted and marched out with his hand on the hilt of his saber.

'Pompous ass,' Major Byrd muttered to himself and shook his head. 'Parading around the fort with a silly-ass saber.'

The angry captain crossed the parade ground accompanied only by his long shadow. Other officers looked away as they passed near Madsen. The captain seethed at the conduct of officers junior to him but turned his eyes neither right nor left.

Waylon Tyson, although a veteran of dozens of such scenes, was sickened. McLeod took one look then turned away. Four bodies lay scalped and mutilated, long shadows of the late afternoon adding to the gruesome nature of the scene.

Sees Far, the Navajo tracker, stood beside Tyson and Johnson. When the two turned, he nodded and used his foot to shake the girl's corpse so the flies lifted away.

'My God!' Johnson covered his mouth.

'Doctor Carpenter was right. He's a mad man. He'll go back for Mrs Mainord,' Tyson said.

Sees Far spoke excellent English but usually chose not to do so. He looked to Tyson and touched his head with two fingers and wiggled his hand like a snake.

Tyson agreed with Sees Far. 'You're right. His mind is crooked. Warped, we would say.'

Johnson finally spoke. 'Who would do such a thing to a child?'

Tyson was surprised that Johnson hadn't made the connection. 'Tell him, Sees Far.'

The Navajo leader used both hands to make an amazingly realistic imitation of a big slow bird settling down on to the bodies.

Johnson was mystified. 'Buzzards? Buzzards didn't do that.'

'No.' Sees Far used one word of English then returned to sign language. He repeated the gesture and added the sign for a man.

'Buzzard Man?' This still made no sense to Johnson.

Tyson explained. 'Buzzard Man. That's the Comanches'

name for Ian Richards. The Navajos picked it up when they traded with the Comanches who slipped into the post.'

Captain Johnson looked stunned once again. 'Richards? My God!'

'He's crazier than I thought.' Johnson was in shock. By force of will the veteran soldier snapped himself out of his daze. 'We have to get him. Which way did he go?'

Sees Far pointed up river toward the west. McLeod swung into the saddle. 'I'm going back. He's on his way to get Carlotta,' he told the captain.

Johnson nodded. 'We'll follow his trail. Sergeant Washington, form a burial detail. Be quick.'

The captain pointed his head toward McLeod. 'That's a tough man, Waylon.'

The lawman nodded. 'I'd hate to have him after me. I'll feel better if he's with Mrs Mainord. He's the one who deserves to get his hands on Richards.'

'Or Mrs Mainord herself,' Johnson added.

TWENTY-THREE

Only the colorful, orange glow above the rock ridges west of the ranch house remained of the sun. The northerly wind gusted while the temperature hovered barely above freezing, a cold that had even more bite because of the rapid drop from almost summer-like conditions two days earlier. Ian Richards was grateful for the heavy, woolen coat that had been in his cache of supplies near the house and congratulated himself again on the perfection of his planning. The Comanchero had spent the last hour watching the blue-coated guards beating their arms and stamping their feet in the cold. After dark he would slip by them and get to the gold coins he had hidden inside his house.

Movement at the house attracted his attention. A buffalo soldier walked briskly to the barn and shortly returned driving Doctor Carpenter's buggy. The heavy oak door in front of his house opened. Richards sat up straighter in surprise. Three people came into view on the porch. He immediately recognized the doctor as he carried his black bag to the buggy. He could see the doctor, who seemed unbothered by the cold wind, smile and nod at the trooper. In the edge of the light he made out Señora Baeza hugging a heavy black shawl around her shoulders. The other figure remained indistinct in the dark shadow of the veranda, but Richards didn't have to see the figure clearly to recognize her.

Ian Richards forgot about the cold. His heart and mind raced as he made his plans. He had already carefully noted the positions of all the guards and knew that getting inside the house would be no problem. When building the house he had known that he might someday need to be able to enter and exit unseen. The guards would never see him.

Ian Richards wanted to hear Carlotta Mainord scream, beg, plead. Pleasure washed over him as he imagined the shock of the guards and that nosy sawbones when they discovered her remains the next day. He would use Carlotta Mainord hard before he got rid of her.

Doctor Carpenter climbed into his buggy and drove away toward the fort. Ian Richards sat calmly honing the blades of his two daggers on a fine finishing stone he carried. The sky was clear. The temperature was going to drop rapidly now that the sunlight was gone, but Ian Richards felt warmer inside than for a long time.

Carlotta and Señora Baeza sat in front of a huge stone fireplace watching the flames jump and cast flickering light. They listened to the fire popping and smelled the rich resin and smoke of high desert piñon. Carlotta worked her fingers nervously in the red shawl in her lap.

Señora Baeza laid a hand on Carlotta's arm. 'Señor McLeod, he is' – she searched unsuccessfully for the words in English – '*muy hombre.*'

Carlotta remained glum. 'Quentin was in no shape to

go out. Now with yesterday's storm and the cold. . . .'
Carlotta's voice trailed away in despair.

'Your Señor McLeod, he will be back.'

'He is a fool to be out there,' Carlotta said, trying to
sound disparaging.

'He is a man in love,' the señora responded softly.

Carlotta shook her head. 'He wanted to get away from
me. I'm tainted goods now.'

The señora squeezed Carlotta's hand. 'If you believe
that, señora, you are the foolish one.'

Near midnight a slender figure dressed in black slipped
from the woods and darted furtively from dark shadow to
dark shadow until he came to the first haystack. Starlight
provided the only dim illumination. The figure dug in the
stack of hay, struck a metallic sound and slid hay away
from a small section of the stack. He raised a small door,
stood watching for movement, then disappeared into the
deep shadow.

Neither Carlotta nor her duenna heard the slight
scraping of the cellar door easing up off the floor in the
kitchen pantry. After looking around for a minute, Ian
Richards raised the door high enough to enter the room.
None of the builders of the house were alive; only Ian
Richards knew the house was built atop one entrance to a
long forgotten Spanish mine.

He guessed that Carlotta would be in the room she had
occupied before. With the light grace of a shadow he
eased to the second door down the hall. Outside he
listened and heard nothing. The door, he knew, would
make no noise. Carefully, soundlessly, he slipped into the
room and closed the door behind him.

In this dim light the shadowy figure appeared even more gaunt and surreal. Smoothly he lifted his dagger out of its scabbard at his side. For several minutes he stood motionless, enjoying the sense of power he felt as he stood over the sleeping woman. He knew that he could kill her at any time, but the dagger used against Carlotta in her sleep would be too quick and painless. He slid it back into its scabbard.

Richards could make out a white towel on the stand by a water pitcher and bowl. Behind him was a brass candlestick. It wasn't necessary for him to look. He had long ago memorized the location of every object in his house. Carefully he wrapped the candlestick in the towel and tested its feel against his hand. He smiled in the dark, raised the cushioned candlestick and brought it sharply down on the head in the bed. Carlotta jerked, grunted slightly and slackened. Casually he put the candlestick down, took a match from the holder in his pocket, struck it and held it high over the woman.

Carlotta was in a blue silk nightgown, her raven hair spread against the white satin bedcover. A tiny spot of red blood oozed from the welt rising on her head. The Englishman touched the match against the wick of the candle stub and shoved the candle back into the brass candlestick. Carlotta lay motionless.

The smile on Ian Richards' face began to twist into a frown. Awkwardly he tilted his head to the side. He shook Carlotta's head gently, then picked up the water pitcher and started to pour. Indecisive, he hesitated and then set the pitcher back into the bowl. Carlotta moaned slightly.

Richards took rawhide strips from his pocket and tied her hands and feet securely to the four bed posts, then tore the towel into strips with which to gag her. Satisfied, he poured more water and wet the remainder of the towel. Very gently he began to bathe Carlotta's face. 'Juliette,' he cooed. 'Wake up, Juliette. Ian's here.'

The Englishman turned away and poured brandy from a decanter into a snifter. Gently he tilted her head and patted small amounts of the brandy under her nose. Her eyes began to flutter. They opened then closed again. They flew wide open, first in disbelief and then in shock at the sight of the Comanchero. Carlotta thrashed back and forth, trying to roll out of bed. She jerked and bucked for several seconds, her eyes desperately seeking some means of escape.

The Englishman stood calmly and patiently, a smile on his face. 'There's no escape, Juliette. You are mine. Mother paid for you.'

Carlotta's eyes flashed. She yanked her arms until the rawhide drew blood. Her eyes and brain grasped for a way to make noise but failed. Richards smiled. In velvety tones he tried to soothe her. 'Juliette. My Juliette, you're all grown up. Your eyes turned blue, Juliette. I don't like that.'

Carlotta lay still, trying desperately to think how to signal the guards.

Richards took a long swallow of the brandy. 'Oh, we're going to have fun again, Juliette, hours of fun, and then you will have to pay for being a slut.' He poured more brandy into the snifter and sipped. 'You ran away from me too many times, Juliette. I can't let you do that again. But we have a whole evening for fun. That and money are what sluts think of anyway, aren't they.'

Carlotta thrashed wildly again but to no avail. Her wrists

bled. Her thrashing made only muffled sounds against the thick feather mattress. Richards drained the snifter and set it aside. The dagger appeared in his hand, his long fingers sensuously caressing the blade. 'You shouldn't have run, Juliette,' he cooed. 'That makes me angry.'

Carlotta's eyes froze on the blade inches from her face. The civilized veneer Ian Richards had shown the world was gone. His eyes shone madly as the point of the dagger lightly touched her nose. He looked in her eyes and laughed, then pressed the point just enough to make a tiny nick in the skin. A small point of blood appeared, pooled, then trickled down her face. 'Juliette. Your raven hair, your blue robe, the white satin . . . all are so much more perfect with a bit of red, blood red.' He moved the knife from her nose to her neck. With his left hand he threw the remaining covers off her. The blue satin of her gown accented the curved lines of her body. 'Such a lovely shade of blue, Juliette.'

He moved the knife lightly to the edge of the blue. The tiniest line of red showed where the knife's point had moved. He hesitated, smiled and slid the blade downward, slicing Carlotta's gown apart. No more blood showed until he paused at her navel. He dug slightly to create another small point of red then sliced the gown to its bottom. 'You are so beautiful, Juliette,' he told her softly as he used the dagger point to move the slit cloth away from her body. He lightly touched her naked leg with his fingers and stroked upwards. He laid the knife on the table and reached to unbutton the top of his shirt.

'Don't move, señor.'

Señora Baeza's voice stunned Carlotta as much as it did Ian Richards. Richards froze then slowly raised his hands in the air, his smile contemptuous.

Señora Baeza held the short pistol in both hands, the barrel pointed at Richards's belly. The muzzle didn't waver.

'Señora Baeza. Please don't point—'

'Quiet!' she hissed, her eyes as hard as obsidian.

'Put the gun down! I—'

The señora dropped the barrel slightly. Fire jumped from the barrel. Ian Richards grabbed his groin as he fell to the floor. He screamed in terror and rage as he held his wound with both hands and thrashed about frantically. Tears rolled down his face. 'She shot me! I'm killed! I—'

Señora Baeza kept the gun muzzle trained on Ian Richards. She cocked the hammer again. The Comanchero froze, his eyes wide in disbelief. 'No! Please don't,' he pleaded, his voice a whine. 'It hurts. Please don't shoot me again.'

His head lay in the door, his left shoulder against the door jamb. Tears ran down his face. 'No, please, señora.'

Señora Baeza's eyes shone with complete contempt upon the groveling Englishman. 'Señor *grande cojones*! Bah.' She took a step backwards and reached for the dagger Ian Richards had left on the table by Carlotta's bed. 'Here, Señora Mainord. I will cut you loose and let you cut the coward's *cojones* away.'

She took the dagger in her left hand and turned slightly to cut Carlotta loose. Carlotta's eyes grew big. She tried to scream.

Ian Richards' hand reached behind his neck. The long fingers grasped his small dagger as the señora cut Carlotta's bonds. Richards hand moved forward.

The heel of a scuffed brown boot pinned Ian Richards's

right hand to the floor. 'Turn loose or I'll crush it,' Quentin McLeod snarled. He shifted his two hundred twenty-five pounds roughly to his heel. Ian Richards attempted to struggle free, Quentin slammed his other heel on the Comanchero's left wrist. Richards screamed but froze in place. The dagger fell to the floor.

Señora Baeza pointed the pistol at Richards. '*Adios, diablo.*'

Quentin McLeod wrapped his big paw around the pistol and pointed it away. 'No!' McLeod told Señora Baeza. He took the pistol and stepped off Richards's hand and wrist. The Comanchero grasped his wound three inches below his groin, just on the inside of his right thigh. 'She's killed me. I'm bleeding to death. You can't just let me bleed to death,' he whined.

Señora Baeza finished cutting Carlotta loose and handed her a robe. Carlotta ignored the robe and threw herself on McLeod, nearly knocking him down.

'I thought you were gone. Oh, God! I thought I had lost you again.' She sobbed deeply.

Quentin hugged her tightly with one arm.

'My leg! Help me. Get the doctor,' the Comanchero pleaded. Several soldiers rushed into the room and grabbed the prisoner.

McLeod and Carlotta held each other tightly in front of the fireplace, the recent distance and coolness gone. Doctor Carpenter stepped into the room. 'I understand you two are all right? Silly question from the looks,' he muttered.

Ian Richards lay on the floor, pleading. The doctor checked him briefly and wrapped a bandage around the leg. 'I can treat him just as well in jail,' he pronounced.

'I don't want to die. Do something!' Richards pleaded to the doctor, who turned back to Richards.

'It's my medical opinion that you'll never die from a gunshot wound.' Doctor Carpenter paused on his way out as he passed Señora Baeza. He took the short revolver that McLeod had returned to him from his bag and offered it to her. 'Would you like to keep this? It seems that you did know how to use it.'

The señora shook her head. 'Keep it, Doctor. But if you use it, be aware. It shoots low and to the left.'

TWENTY-FOUR

Fort Sumner was buzzing over the capture of Ian Richards. Waylon Tyson had deposited him in the same cell recently occupied by Quentin McLeod.

Fort Sumner was now getting ready for its most celebrated wedding ever. Carlotta had agreed that since McLeod had thrown away his Yankee pants, she would marry him. Doctor Carpenter had agreed to give the bride away but offered his opinion that, in their present condition, no one should expect too much of a honeymoon.

Captain Madsen slunk around like a whipped dog. If Madsen's career had not been as dead as Oliver Loving described it during the trial, it certainly was now. Madsen went about his duty but officers, enlisted men, and civilians alike treated him as if he was invisible.

'How badly would you like to get out of here, Ian?'

Richards lay silent for a moment and then rose with the grace of a mountain lion. Already he showed no ill effects of having been shot by Señora Baeza. The Comanchero walked up to Madsen and grasped the bars, long fingers circling and squeezing the steel. His eyes locked into Madsen's. Madsen had never been comfortable around the Englishman. He averted his eyes from the intense gaze.

'Name it,' Richards answered eagerly. 'Anything!'

Madsen already looked older since Quentin McLeod's trial. Puffiness around his eyes and face was more noticeable. Now his face was eager as he answered the Comanchero, his voice low and tight with bitterness, 'You can escape and leave here a wealthy man. We can get even with these people and get away at the same time.'

'Whatever,' Richards hissed.

'The army payroll for the Department of New Mexico is in the safe here. There's more than $50,000. I can take the payroll by myself, but I need you to get across the Staked Plains. The Comanches are more stirred up than ever.'

Ian Richards leaned forward until his thin face was between the bars. 'We can make it – easily.'

Madsen fished the key from a pocket. 'I also have two dozen Spencers from the arsenal that we can use to trade with the Comanches.'

'Let me out,' Richards urged.

Madsen hesitated for only a moment before he unlocked the door. 'Wait here,' he told Richards. He looked into the jail office and then waved Richards on.

'My weapons,' Richards demanded.

Madsen swung open a cabinet door to reveal Richards's rifle, pistol, cartridge belt and the deadly double-edged daggers. Richards fondly caressed his knives.

Madsen fumbled with the tumblers to the safe, stopped and started several times. Ian Richards looked out the window several times. He slid his dagger part of the way out of the scabbard several times, fidgeted and sighed.

'Blasted hell!' Richards finally exploded.

Madsen looked up at the Comanchero, wiped the sweat from his brow, and took a slip of paper from his pocket. He fumbled again then finally opened the door. The two men wrestled the single strongbox out of the safe and lugged it outside.

'I have horses and mules behind Ethan Thompson's,' Madsen told his new partner. 'He goes home every day for dinner and a siesta.'

Madsen and Richards made their way unseen to Ethan Thompson's by staying in the alley behind the few store buildings. One mule was already packed with the rifles. Another waited, ready to haul gold. They quickly transferred the gold into panniers made to pack on mules. The Comanchero lifted them on to the pack frames and lashed them into place. Madsen stood watching as Ian Richards tied the packs. 'Horses are inside,' he told Richards, his voice tight with excitement.

Inside, Madsen untied his horse and turned toward the door to mount, but drew up in shock when he found Ian Richards facing him, his dagger drawn. 'You told me why *you* need *me*, Madsen,' Richards said. 'You didn't tell me why *I* need you now that I'm free and have the gold.'

'But I freed you,' Madsen pleaded. 'I got the gold.'

'Loving was right,' Richards hissed. 'You're an incompetent fool.' He smiled malevolently then flicked his wrist so quickly that Madsen didn't even see it move. His body fell to the floor, blood gushing from his slit throat. Richards took a moment to slash his face several times and then wipe his knife clean. He quickly added Madsen's saddle horse to the string of pack mules. He swung gracefully into the saddle of his own long-legged bay and headed out of the stable into the corral.

Just as he emerged into the sunlight, he yanked the bay's reins up in surprise as he came upon Carlotta and McLeod strolling hand in hand. McLeod slapped his hip for the Colt, remembering with a sinking feeling that he hadn't put it on before leaving the house. He lunged at Richards and tried to drag him from his saddle.

Richards kicked his boot out from his stirrup and knocked McLeod away. As McLeod fell backwards, he grabbed at Richards. He missed, but came away with the rawhide riata.

Richards fought to get control of the dancing bay without dropping the lead line to the mules. McLeod quickly built a loop in the Comanchero's rope. Richards fought his plunging horse to a momentary standstill and raised his pistol, his face lit by a fierce grin of triumph. The pistol spurted fire and smoke. McLeod's head snapped back; he spun to the ground, the rope falling on top of him. Richards waved the pistol in the air like a Comanche waving a bloody scalp in triumph.

For a moment he stared at Carlotta. His eyes glazed a bit. 'Juliette,' he began. He yanked his head toward town where people were coming into the street looking for the source of the gunshot. One man pointed toward the stables. Others followed his gesture. Several shouted.

Ian Richards looked back toward Carlotta then spurred his horse toward the corral gate and the Staked Plains.

Carlotta stood stunned into inaction for a moment, then grabbed for the riata McLeod had dropped. She threw the loop desperately toward Richards. The loop flew high over the cross post of the corral gate and settled around Ian Richards's neck. Carlotta squatted and dug her heels into the dirt as the rope snapped taut. Richards jerked backwards. The horse snorted and danced away. Ian Richards hung suspended from the high crosspiece of the gate.

Carlotta felt the rope slipping from her hands. Desperate, she dove for the snubbing post in the middle of the corral and struggled to wrap the rope around it. The rope burned her hands but she held tightly to it.

She felt hands on top of hers and jerked her head around to find McLeod helping her hold the rope. Blood streamed down the side of his head from the shallow groove cut by Richards's bullet. Together they dallied the rope around the post and tied it securely.

Ian Richards's body spun toward Carlotta; his hands grasped at the rope in reflex, then relaxed and fell to his side. His neck bent sharply to the side. His lifeless eyes faced the Staked Plains as his body swung back and forth in the wind.

'I'm free,' Carlotta told McLeod. 'For the first time since that man touched me, I'm really free.'